An Ill Wind Blows

To Dea and Penelope (ha ha) ~
Hope you are blown away
by adventure!

An Ill Wind Blows

Written and
illustrated by

Lori R. Lopez

Let's break some crayons! ♥

Love, *Lori R. Lopez*

Author's Draft

Trilllogic Innoventions

AN ILL WIND BLOWS
Written and illustrated by
LORI R. LOPEZ

First printed by
Create Space

This is a work of fiction.

ISBN: 1484097734
EAN-13: 978-1484097731

First Edition 2013
Printed in U.S.A.

The unique adventure AN ILL WIND BLOWS depicts one night when an ordinary person lacking confidence must battle a wicked wind. The stakes are high as she, along with friends and foes, travels through a magical storm world that culminates in a ghost town populated by more than just spirits. This is a story that keeps delivering action and fun throughout. It is more than a single tale in a single genre. The book blends Humor, Horror, and Fantasy.

From the time the characters are sucked into the storm, the reader is transported with them on a strange chaotic trek. Meezly finds herself tangled in a web of chills and intrigue as she attempts to search for a mysterious gem called The Cursed Eye, which her missing father entrusted her to safeguard. The stone was used by a Sumerian king to transform an evil jinn from a wind spirit to a vainglorious force.

This fable is as imaginative and unconventional in style as it is in plot. A vulnerable individual struggling to overcome debilitating losses, Meezly stumbles through a gauntlet of thirteen macabre tribulations down a forest highway. Twists and madness abound during her eclectic hectic journey of the soul. It is a lighthearted yet touching trek that readers will want to take again.

What is an Author's Draft? It is an original concept devised by Lori R. Lopez. Much like a Director's Cut in film, it is the author's true voice, the author's pure and untampered vision!

S.I.C.
(Spelling Is Correct)

Please note that I am a creative author and as such prefer to spell, punctuate, and use words as I please.

For the child in us all

Terms thrust like swords and daggers
Tossed careless to the wind
The rot-mottish curse of braggers
That stings the thickest-skinned
~ "Bon-Mottery" by Lori R. Lopez

An ill wind blows no good. ~ Proverb

BOOK ONE

THE DEMON WIND

1

THE MOST EXTREME MOMENTS can sneak up on you
when you least expect. Suddenly, *wham,* they're right
in your face — and you're helpless to prevent them.
That has been my experience since I was very small.
Things just seemed to happen. There was nothing
I could do about it but accept whatever came. Like
standing in the path of the wildest wickedest storm that
ever blew. Or on some other catastrophic collision course.
You simply knew it was Fate. And Fate could be one
out-of-control unholy carnival of terror!

My name is Arletta Trimble. I'll be your guide for
this journey through the darkest night of my existence.
And probably yours too, unless you're used to stepping
off the edge into absolute craziness. I don't mean the
kind that inhabits a rubber playroom where the toys
have been dented and gnawed by sets of permanent
teeth. I'm talking mind-warping bizarre. The stuff
of nightmares and hallucinations.

As I recall, I was sitting there minding my own
beeswax when along came a wind that ripped the
back door from the building where I lived. It snagged
grouchy Ben Doogan right with it. He takes care
of maintenance around here. Well, he used to.
They never did find him. Once the door was gone,
I had no choice but to poke my nose into the situation.
It isn't that I'm snoopy like some people think. I'm just
naturally curious. Which tends to make me prone to
an abundance of problems, because following your nose
can be a dangerous proposition.

On this particular afternoon, that was precisely the case. I should know. I'm gifted that way. My mother said I could smell trouble a mile away. I don't like to brag, but I think it's more like ten miles.

There I was, morally inclined to explore the event. How could I have guessed it would lead to such diabolical disaster? Well, I could have and should have and did. And that's one reason I had to investigate.

Another excuse, I was on a mission. A quest of sorts. In fact, a treasure hunt.

You must think I'm exaggerating, that this sounds rather melodramatic. I wish I could say you're right but frankly, you couldn't be more wrong. If that's what you were thinking. If you weren't then you weren't wrong. You also weren't right. You weren't thinking, period.

You *have* to be wondering what kind of treasure I was after! It wasn't a big cache of gold or anything. It was a stone. And not some gaudy gem; a plain unpolished unfaceted mineral, although it was called The Cursed Eye. Also The Evil Eye. It was even translated as The Jaded Eye, perhaps because it was purported to glow a lovely jade-green when activated.

The stone had been discovered clutched in the fist of an ancient Sumerian king — who, it was believed, wrested it out of the mitts of a high-priest attempting to overthrow him. The rivals stabbed each other to death. The king's reign lasted roughly a total of fifteen minutes. His name was never recorded in Cuneiform glyphs, thus history books failed to honor him.

The Eye was credited with supernatural properties. However, no amount of spitting and buffing or uttering phrases or rapping and jostling would get it to shine — to wield its power, a tremendous force that could be used as a weapon — and subsequent owners sold or bequeathed it as a mere novelty.

You may be acquainted with similar tales about magical stones. Versions of the legend floated around for ages, appearing on most if not every continent. But this is the point of origin that such myths were based upon.

Original or not, it was the same old story of greed, ambition, and men wanting to rule the world. You know the type. There are generally one or two lurking at the bottom of every great adventure. And that's what this is. A terrifyingly twisted adventure. So hang on to your hat! If you don't have a hat, you'd better get one. This is going to be a breezy ride . . .

I suppose I should mention how I learned of the stone and why I was intent on locating it. My father's sister Camille dropped by for a visit to deliver a packet of documents from the attorney for the family estate. My parents disappeared a year earlier when their rented jeep smashed through a guardrail into a canyon. The road had been wet; they were traveling a remote mountainous region and were presumed dead. I was very shaken and appreciated Aunt Camille's support after the tragedy. She was my closest living relative. My only living relative. She was handling the legal issues and loose ends on my behalf.

These papers she brought were not financial in scope. There were no bills or invoices or bank statements. It was a list of assets that my aunt assured me needed to be liquidated to cover my expenses. She wanted to know where to find an item that had been inventoried but was missing — catalogued as a "precious stone of Sumer, The Cursed Eye".

"Never heard of it," I shrugged. My parents were collectors of antiquities and artifacts. I couldn't keep up with their purchases. The thing sounded like bad news, unlucky. I wondered if it might be responsible for their accident. Flinching, I told her that if she found the relic to please get rid of it.

"I promise I will," she pledged. "Are you sure you don't remember seeing a pretty jewel?"

I shook my head. It was lunchtime. "Would you care for a fruit cup?" I offered, wiggling my itchy nose with a finger.

Camille had an appointment and was running late. "If you think of where it might be, let me know," she insisted.

An envelope drifted to my lap as my aunt crammed the sheaf of pages into a mega-sized shopping-bag purse. "What's this?" My name was handwritten on the front; my nickname, to be exact: *Meezly*, as in "measly" . . . that's how my parents and friends referred to me. I was premature at birth and stayed petite in stature, whereas my folks had been quite lanky. Mom and Dad joshed and teased a lot, and it was their style of endearment.

Aunt Camille, who was tall herself, used Arletta. It always seemed a bit formal. She glanced down, impatient to leave. "I haven't the foggiest," she clucked. "I went over those papers myself." Like the claw of a robot, her hand darted to nab the envelope. "Give me that. You needn't worry."

"It's addressed to me." Resisting, I opened the sealed flap and unfolded a sheet of stationery containing a decorous border. Thin lines of script filled both sides. The letter, signed "Dad", was dated just days before my parents embarked on their final trip.

Tears hampered my vision. A trembling hand further impaired the ability to read. "Darling daughter," penned my father, "should anything befall your mother and me while we are away, there is something you need to know. Strange occurrences have trailed us ever since Morocco." He described encountering the stone at a curio shoppe in a bazaar; the merchant's elaborate sales pitch. The legend intrigued them. Until their ship nearly sank then their plane almost crashed in virulent storms.

"Your mother fears the object is truly cursed.
I do not believe so. There is something else, something
heinous shadowing us. It is my suspicion that whatever
it is seeks The Eye and must not be allowed to claim it.
This is important. Hide the stone!"

I was shocked at these words, a plea from my dad,
belatedly conveyed to me by random circumstance.
My expression mirrored the emotion.

"What is it?" Aunt Camille pilfered the page out
of my fingers. Avid eyes skimmed the lines, her forehead
furrowed. "You're lying!" she accused. "According to this,
you know where the jewel is!"

"How could I when I've only just heard of it now?"
I protested.

She was unconvinced. My doting aunt, for the
briefest interlude, unmasked a harsh snippy demeanor
behind her typical syrupy exterior. "You said yourself
you don't want it. Tell me where it is!" she pried. "Your
father's letter is proof that it needs to be disposed of."

My stomach growled as if in response. "It's
lunchtime," I repeated, absently rubbing my nose.
"Are you staying or not?"

The sweetness returned. "You know how much
I care," Camille amended. "I'll be back later." A last
appeal as she hurried off: "Try to remember where
it could be!"

"I don't know!" Why wouldn't she listen?

Eating my lunch, I mulled the letter's warning.
And was appalled to realize that Camille had taken the
note! I had an empty envelope! This irritated me no end.
What right did she have to confiscate a letter composed
exclusively for me? I hated to be ungrateful, after all
Camille had done to help, but there were times that
I had to question whose side she was on!

The more I contemplated what my father wrote,
the more uneasy I felt about the scene with my aunt.
What had gotten her in such a frenzy?

Was there indeed a curse that had settled over my family?

I grew determined to get answers. The logical place to start was with the stone. Wherever it was, and *whatever*, I needed to find it.

When the rear door was torn away, I had entered the hallway dressed for an excursion. I didn't go out much, preferring the indoors. It was safer. I had lost my confidence the previous year and took sedatives daily to soothe my anxiety, prescribed by Doctor Hurst, a friend of my aunt's. Normally I drank them with lunch.

I skipped the pills, poured them in the sink after Camille's departure. I wanted to be alert, on my toes. The medication rendered me *too* relaxed, even groggy.

That day I had made up my mind and nothing was going to stop me. The stone must be somewhere within reach, or Father wouldn't have urged me to hide it. The one thing I didn't glean from his letter was what it looked like.

Donning a burgundy beret, dark fleece jacket, and my customary single-strap navy-blue messenger bag, I stole from my domicile in a futile effort to avert being inspected by peeping neighbors.

Missus Drager — The Dragon Lady — was already ogling me through the crack of her door. Choking on a whiff of the sickeningly floral fragrance that emanated in waves, crossing hazel orbs at the intrusive blinking eyeball, I hastened toward the back of the building. I was on the ground floor. No stairs to risk meeting unfriendlies. Just a gauntlet of eyes. I swigged contaminated oxygen and strode by.

Spiro Viscotti's gaze, steely brown accented by thick hairy caterpillars, chiseled into my periphery. The guy, who had an ulterior motive for anything he said and did, whispered in a moping manner to have a fortuitous day. *What was that about?* I frowned.

Driscoll Wunderbar — a doughy man who shaved then polished his head and face (including the eyebrows) so they gleamed — slouched in his doorway wearing an insolent smirk. I ignored him.

Farther down the dim lengthy tunnel I paused, discerning a scuff; the rustle of clothing; a faint creak.

Next to Mister Gourd's abode, I froze at the sight of custodian Ben Doogan pushing the door and being jerked off his feet. In a flash the hinges caved and he was gone, quaffed by a vortex of visible fury.

No world remained outside the vacant rectangle, only a mass of swirling.

Mister Gourd, a towering nefarious figure, joined me in the corridor. I was too stunned at that instant to feel my usual fright of the sinister spying wraith . . . who seemed to appear out of nowhere and just always be there.

We exchanged glances. I captured a mental snapshot. Piercing sharp features. A dense crop of black and silver hair. A scarred groove above his eyes.

The atmosphere of the hall began to pull me, atom by atom, then molecules. Mister Gourd clinched my arm and hauled me in a perpendicular direction. I was being dragged forward and laterally and couldn't decide to which I should yield. I was scared either way.

With a yell and a vicious yank, Mister Gourd won. I lurched into his lair, coughing as if the breath had been squeezed out of my lungs. We sprawled on the floor, woodenly tumbling.

My grim savior extended a hand. I rose to my feet, aided by the brooding specter. Did I owe him a thank-you? I awkwardly puzzled.

We watched with surprise as three tenants whizzed by in a blur. I almost thought my aunt and her friend Nigel Hurst somersaulted past as well.

Mister Gourd plunked me onto an upholstered chair. My head was dizzy, yet I didn't care to be treated in such a rude fashion. The villainous rogue pensively regarded me. Was he deliberating what instrument or method to use for my murder?

His stance blocked my escape from the confined quarters. I nervously gagged. Hysteria was rising. The uncanny phenomenon in the hall could not be worse than the fact I was being held prisoner! Most homicides were perpetrated by somebody known to the victim. That's what they said on T.V.

I view a lot of television. I also read a lot of books. My favorite tome is the dictionary. So many words, arranged in alphabetic order. Everything neat and tidy and clear. If you didn't understand a word in a definition, you could conveniently flip pages and look that one up too. It made perfect sense.

Unlike my life. Nothing about that made sense anymore. My parents were gone. My serene organized existence had been uprooted. Overnight it had revised completely. How could anyone feel safe in a world where such a rapid degree of disruption was possible?

I couldn't, that was for sure. And here I was, thrust into another abrupt alternate universe, my tentative foothold on security and stability being swept out from under me again.

Perhaps this explanation will enable you to comprehend the incomprehensible: why I would choose to fling myself beyond a familiar menace into an entirely unknown situation. What did I have to lose? At least it would satisfy curiosity and appease my disquiet. I might continue the expedition. There was even a chance that the ruckus in the corridor wasn't as bad as it seemed.

Presented with a Fight Versus Flight option, I picked the latter. I was no heavyweight contender. And Mister Gourd was spookier than a passage leading to a bunch of wind.

So I hurled past my ghoulish captor and was immediately whisked from the building into the spurling jaws and gullet of a raging cyclone.

Into The Storm

2

THE WIND DEVIL chortled, having absorbed his target —
along with various strays. Devouring the girl was easy.
Whole villages had been consumed in pursuit of others.
He refused to serve these humble beings, and to ensure
that he would never be compelled to, he had traced the
stone as it changed hands through his connection to
a new master. Whoever acquired The Eye possessed
dominion over him and could issue commands. Except
that the stone must deem the individual worthy.

It aggravated him that this paltry female had
influence! The Eye's aura was linked strongly to hers.
Human life was frail and could be snuffed out like
a flame in a single puff. Yet the jinn of mistrals sought
freedom — to guide his own destiny — and therefore
needed to control the stone so none could rule him.
He needed the girl for that.

The storm demon was old as the universe. As were
all spirits whether good or evil, mortal or immortal; all
sparks of essence that recycled in the many evolving
infinite forms of life. Ancients labeled him an Ekimmu.
To them he was known as Anzillu: *Abomination*.

When the stone was unearthed — its potential
revealed by a prophet — and the king's high-priest
evoked him, amplifying his force through enchantment,
he was summoned as Ara-Alal-Alad (Screaming Destroyer
and Protector); Ara-Ab-Zu (Limitless Howl); and Ara-Apsu
(The Howling Abyss).

Not *one* who endeavored to harness him was approved by the rock since the king. Until this girl. She was a thorn, a pustulent canker. That so flimsy a creature might have him in her thrall was an insult and a threat, for The Eye could be used to rescind his superior powers and reduce him to air!

The blowhard was in a foul mood, banging clouds together with his rancor to rain a torrent of drops and thunderbolts. Churning a hurricane of enmity as he amused himself with his conquest. Anzillu would break and batter and obliterate her, to his malevolent soul's content.

3

THE AIR WAS CALMER inside. My hurtle plopped me
to a bed of construction debris, bones, limbs and torsos,
in what I perceived as the belly of the beast. The tranquil
zone at the heart of a storm is considered *the eye*, as if
each blast of weather resembles a mythical cyclops.
This infernal pit where I had landed could not be termed
anything but an ogre's gut. Strewn about me were bodies
galore, like I had fallen into a giant cannibal's pot — by
way of his throat!

     Among the recent acquisitions to the stew melee
stirred several wretches in my condition, still in one piece
but rattled and unkempt. I recognized them as the four
neighbors I avoided like contagion. *Fantastic!* I inwardly
moaned.

     Mister Gourd must have chased me. The conclusion
increased my paranoia and distrust. I crawled out of
range so he couldn't grab my neck. It didn't count that
we were literally in the same mess.

     Driscoll Wunderbar brushed detritus off his domed
scalp and shot me a glare. His flabby frame wallowed in
the congestion, striving to gain his feet.

     Spiro Viscotti haughtily snorted, wiry and
pseudo-cool; his bleach-blond hair, weasel face, white
teeshirt and khakis marred by the mire.

     Missus Drager (I think her first name was Mindy,
but Dragon Lady was so much more appropriate)
scrambled up by pawing at those around her, living
or deceased. "This is your fault!" she hissed, impaling
me with a grimace.

Excuse me for living! I sarcastically reflected.
I didn't need to get involved in a debate about blame.
Or, for that matter, to speculate if we were aboard an
alien spacecraft. Not that my mind wasn't receptive
to the notion.

     I was busy calculating which direction was out.
I had a mission to fulfill . . . and planned to leave no
stone unturned until the stone was uncovered that
I was asked to conceal.

     I traipsed off, neverminding that twisters didn't
actually scarf up people and gurgitate them. Reality
could be weird. Grisly at times. Some days it rained
dead birds. Being in the stomach of a windstorm
might be queer, but apparently it could happen.

     Venturing along a glisterous curving shaft,
I entered a chamber where a lake had been slurped
from its bed and stored like a fishbowl. Aquatic life
swam or floated in the water. But there was no glass,
just air between the edge of the lake and me!

     Marveling at the anomaly, I ambled to an adjacent
vault. Here there was a gabble of ducks and geese
honking and quacking. "Odd," I muttered.

     The next niche (or stomach) hosted a nursery of
baby squids and octopuses frolicking merrily on the
"floor": arm-wrestling, patty-caking, drumming or
tap-dancing — I couldn't tell which.

     There was a rainbow room of colorful fowl:
cardinals and quetzals, macaws and lorikeets,
parrots and peacocks.

     Another vault thrummed with hummingbirds
and locusts, pigeons and crickets.

     An aviary trilled: songbirds fluttering and roosting,
stacked in vertical columns.

     Chipmunks, squirrels, and gophers frisked; rabbits
and hares were ensconced in a large spherical pen.

     Fresh and saltwater fish flitted within a water-drop
aquarium.

The funnel cloud exhibited a cluster of lost balloons, a den of orange and snow foxes, a clash of cats and dogs. I beheld a white cow with no spots, a dark horse, a carousel pony, a sheepish lamb, and a kangaroo. The farm animals complacently masticated, yet there was no grass.

I gawped at hordes of frogs, worms, spiders, anemones, ladybugs, crows, salamanders and serpents; vaults teeming with a specific category or class, ready to be unloaded above an unsuspecting town. It gave new meaning to the expression *Don't rain on my parade*.

It was a zoo without the cages. Assorted cavities and blobs displaying any number of pastoral, marine, mundane or exotic sideshow attractions.

Despite my preoccupation with locating the stone, I couldn't help fretting that munitions were being stocked for a war against humanity. An Armageddon battle of supremacy. It sounded ridiculous. How long had the gale been cavorting, dispensing bombs that squirmed, raiding then unleashing these arsenals? Were there multiple maniacal storms? How did it gather a single species? What could it want? And why me? Why my neighbors?

On top of these perplexities, I was struggling to maintain my resolve, what little courage I had mustered. I wanted to carry out my father's request. It was a solemn oath. But I hadn't gone anywhere by myself in months and my confidence — what confidence? I had bolstered myself with a shallow reserve of fortitude, based on eagerness and a tremulous will, the fleet bravado of a paper lion.

Breath labored. Anxiety gripped my chest, strangling my heart. "I can't do this alone!" I gasped.

"Who says you're alone?" A cheerful aspect hove into my perception.

"Tonka!" I was delighted to see him.

The middle-aged jovial man clasped one of my hands in both of his; a finger sandwich, he liked to jest. He was a glib fellow sporting a black low-crowned flat-topped brim who didn't talk about himself. There was nothing to tell. He had lost his past along with his memory. Tonka was all he could recall — the brand of his favorite toy when he was a child. He bowed and relinquished my hand.

"Would we let you leave widout us?" laughed Juniper. The ebony woman's melodic voice and accented diction rang like music to my ears as she looped her arm with mine.

"Junebug!" I gleefully exclaimed. That's what I called her for short, though the nickname had an equal amount of letters as her regular one, which was a translation of her African moniker: Mreteni. Every child in her family was named for a tree, she had informed me.

"You know we're always here for you, Meezly!" A girl with purple and black hair, dressed in a red teeshirt and matching jeans, crimson high-top sneakers on her feet, gave me a tight hug.

"Rhonda!" I greeted. "Thanks." She was like a sister.

"Ah, you know me. I'm gonna butt in. That's how I am. You can't get rid of me. So don't even try!" Unlike Tonka, Ronnie liked to talk about herself.

"Okay, I won't." I gave her a teasing shove.

"Arf, arf."

"Rupert!" I hugged my fourth best friend, a skinny geek with a kinky orange mop who liked to pretend he was a dog. It was his thing, the way Rhonda dyed half of her hair purple and only wore red, Tonka was a contrast of average and mysterious, and Juniper had a practical solution for everything except her problems. Rupert's true identity was Terence.

These were my buddies, and I was so glad to see them. My eyes brimmed with tears. The happy kind.

"We noticed the storm while we were in the garden. People were flying into it. We thought you might need some help." Tonka winked.

"There was noding else to do but run to da wind," Junebug stated.

"It was my idea to jump!" boasted Rhonda.

"Arf." Rupert grinned, panting with his tongue out. "We're here for ya, Grace." He sometimes called me that.

I ruffled his shaggy mane and beamed. "You guys are terrific! What would I do without you?"

"Turn into a basket-case?" suggested Ronnie.

Lolloping her arm lightly, I agreed that I would be in sorry shape.

"The reason I'm here," I told them, "aside from being scooped up in a tornado, is that I'm on a treasure quest. I'm searching for a stone."

"Arf, arf!" Rupert excitedly pranced (on two legs; he wasn't a *real* dog) to a chamber in which nestled a trove of smooth river rocks.

"Not just any stone," I clarified.

"Errrr." Rupert hung his head.

"What does it look like?" Rhonda was noisily chomping gum and tugged at it with her fingers. Gross. She didn't wash her hands. And wiped the saliva on her baggy red jeans. It isn't as nasty as leaving the gum overnight on the wall or bedpost or table, then munching it some more, which she probably did too. I never said she was perfect. Friends can be annoying.

"That's the thing. I don't know," I admitted, wishing she would jettison the gum. Of course, then I would probably step in it.

"So you're on an *impossible* quest." Rhonda snickered, stretching the gray wad like elastic.

"How many days have you been chewing that?" I had to ask.

"Three." The girl nibbled it back into her mouth.

I know what you're thinking: Why should I care about personal habits when I've been swallowed by the wind? You make a good point. But my world had been off-kilter for a year! Technicalities and priorities need not apply. Rational perspectives went out the window. I didn't care if this was an alien vessel, an allergic reaction to Missus Drager's perfume, or a seriously bad case of indigestion! My emotional balance was wobbling to and fro, veering from an inflated ego and the yearning to perform a noble task to being meek and phobic and crippled.

The staunch company of friends buoyed my spirit, however. We were a band of intrepid wanderers, sallying forth on . . . well, more than an adventure. My father said it was important. His tone seemed urgent. I was ignorant that the evil he warned of — the curse my mother was afraid of — could be the very obstacle surrounding me. I had walked straight into its trap.

4

THE DETESTED NEIGHBORS glowered at each other
and clumsily attempted to exit the tombish vault.
Bumping shoulders, they stumbled to a tubal avenue
with similar alcoves then leerily swapped stares.

The quartet desired to separate, but there was
no intersection permitting each to diverge. Also, they
entertained a common goal. The pack wound up
scurrying in unison after the girl, who served as the
catalyst for them being there. It wasn't revenge they
coveted. Nor any neighborly attachment. These tenants,
primarily churlish slugs, intended to skulk in her wake
for their own secret purposes.

As three had stealthily accomplished in that
distant corridor, they tiptoed casually with obvious
postures. Mister Gourd passively followed, rolling his
eyes at the feigned nonchalance of those before him.

Arriving at a bend, the trio hesitated and projected
their noggins in varying heights around the mist that
comprised a wall. Gourd groaned, sauntering by the
furtive slinkers with an attitude of disdain.

They huffily caught up, elbowing past him to
resume their clandestince.

Gourd whistled idly between his teeth.

Driscoll, Spiro, and Drager twirled as one . . .
forefingers to lips . . . and succinctly cautioned,
"SSSHHHHHH!!!"

The whistling ceased. Mister Gourd's mouth
twitched.

Like a farcical stage production, nobody commented on the absurdity of hiking through the organs and arteries of a demonic tempest. Suspension of disbelief had been invoked, as if it were an ordinary situation.

Mister Gourd himself, whose first name was Richard, preferred to keep a broad mind concerning most topics and events. He had glimpsed too many horrors, and survived too many torments, to let a wacky maelstrom of malignant air contort his view of the cosmos.

What was the worst that could happen? He asked himself that when confronted with any challenge. His answer; the only answer: There are worse things than dying.

He should know. He had committed them. Just about every sin in the book. Every excuse to slow-cook in a boiling vat of oil, fry to a crisp on a gasoline-soaked grill, sear to cinders on a funeral-pyre hot tin roof. He had done it all, or almost. And egressed unscathed from the conflagration, marching tattered and sooty up from the gates of Hell.

Hacking out smoke and carbon, filling singed lungs with a smoggy draught of air (which rhymes with "naught" in *my* book and signifies the opposite of a draft), he had gritted his teeth and gone right back.

Sure, there were some scars. A few dings and bullet-holes. The sheen of despair on his face, and the soulless abjectivity of a man without compunction in the cold numb eyes of a man who wore his stained-glass conscience on his sleeve.

He had watched the life crushed out of women and children underneath the boot heels and tank treads and explosions of men killing or subjugating men. He had seen houses strafed with ammo rounds like drive-by shootings, and heard the screams of the innocent as the strong arm of the law laid it down with undue absolute authority.

He had witnessed the slaughter, the bloodshed,
the violence and misery of foreign and civil wars. He had
done his share of throat-slitting and gun-baths, defending
or aggressing, gaining an inch but taking a mile.

And with every atrocity, his membrane of apathy
had toughened to a suit of armor. His heart became
more calloused, his vision less distinct. Yet his hand
now wavered when he aimed the barrel. His teeth
clenched asleep or awake; there was a constant ache
in his jaw. His brain fixated on the garish coruscations,
the stony fields of regret. But there was no going back
to atone for what he'd done. He could only wade forward
through a rising tide of anguish and suffering.

Richard Gourd had seen too much, loved too deeply,
and sorrowed too hard. For all that he was and wasn't,
and could never be again, he mourned. But he couldn't
sob. That capacity had been steamrollered out of him.

It was a volatile man who couldn't weep. A man
on the brink.

5

I WAS UNAWARE that my movements were of such
interest to persons of such little interest to me. For
someone with a sixth sense about trouble, I could be
fairly oblivious.

   I didn't realize what a crazy corner my life had
turned, that it defied the physical and mental parameters
of what Science and Society defined as Normal. I was
too close to the madness.

   Anyway, there are a million kinds of Normal.
Maybe a billion. But I believe there are certain things
you just have to accept as basic, irrefutable. A standard
for all else — the myriad deviations and possibilities —
to be compared. Not judged, merely established as
a reference point. Without an inkling of where North
lies, without a Prime Meridian or Equator, we can't tell
if we're East or West or South. We can't gauge what is
up unless we know what is down. And we cannot know
who we are if we do not understand how or where we
started. Normal is necessary.

   Like the division between Normal and Abnormal,
there once existed a line between Real and Fantasy
in my consciousness. My material province also.
The border was vital in order to distinguish sense
from nonsense, fact from fiction, sanity from lunacy.

   As with Normal, there are all kinds of Crazy.

   I don't mean the phobias or health disorders that
any one of us might succumb to and still be lucid. I'm
talking bonkers. Too far gone. When a birdy pops out
and chimes "Cuckoo, cuckoo!" in your cranium.

On the day of the tornado, that line had been erased. My friends and I weren't roaming through a parallel dimension. We hadn't left our world. We had been ingested by a world within a world . . . a mammoth creep-show circus tent of trouble. That's a lot of trouble.

In my kookiest imaginings, I never contrived that I would meet a living breathing storm. That was too outside the boundaries of convention. Monsters were supposed to have flesh and blood, hair and teeth and claws — not wind-chill factors, bluster, hail, turbulence, and corkscrews!

Yet here I was trekking through the nucleus of a monstrous squall with four of the nicest people on the planet. More correctly, I trekked while Rhonda skipped and Rupert gallivanted. Juniper sedately strolled.

The enigmatic Tonka plodded by placing each foot in front of the other, as if traversing a narrow bridge or cable.

"Were you a tightrope walker?" I guessed. It was a game we played.

He didn't think so.

"A mime?" I quizzed.

He spread his hands in a bewildered gesture, visage sad.

"A clown? I love clowns!" I gaily reckoned.

Tonka poked his chest with a thumb. So did he. Though he didn't know if he had been one. He doffed his black brim hat, then tamped it on his head again.

It dawned on me that we were like Dorothy Gale in the land of Oz with The Scarecrow, Tin Man, and Lion. Rupert was Toto. If we met a Wizard, Tonka could ask for his memory. Rupert, a tail. Rhonda? I hadn't a clue.

"Hey, what would you ask for if this was Oz?" I demanded.

She peered into my eyes, visually dredging my depths.

It tickled. I squealed, "Don't look at *me*, I don't know!"

We laughed.

"A new stick of gum," I intuited. "Am I right?"

She nodded, grinning. "I accidentally swallowed it."

I turned to Junebug, my eyebrows elevated. "Your stone, girl. Dat is what we came here for! Den you could wish us home."

She always had the ideal advice. Conversely, I felt disappointed. This wasn't Oz. It wasn't Kansas either. We had been transported by a twister. That much was the same. But this was no dream. At least, I didn't think it was. I pinched Ronnie's arm.

"Ouch! What was that for?" she yelped.

"Just checking."

Rhonda socked my arm.

"Ow!" Nope, neither of us were dreaming.

We had halted near an archway. The passage widened on the other side. There was an odor, the stench of decay. My nose wrinkled. "Wait, guys. There's something wrong."

Adrenaline surged. My emotions plummeted in a clammy nauseating descent. I desperately wanted to go back the way we had come!

Rupert barked, then growled at something beyond. I dove to restrain him and missed. Baying, the nerdy lad barged through the entrance.

We were impelled to join him. The air thickened as I crossed the threshold; the atmosphere was gloomier, the way it feels when black clouds assemble in the sky. Vaporous banks loomed above, rippling and writhing, seething with turgid cargo.

Distracted, I stepped on a squishy lump.

And winced at the floor.

My foot, clad in a loafer, recoiled from a dead bird. The ground was littered with small feathered corpses. Blackbirds with crooked necks, feet jutting, toes curled.

A crackle of thunder. Electricity flared. We were inundated by a deluge of water, mingled with — *blood!* Shielding our faces, hands splayed, palms uplifted to ward off the downpour, the five of us braced to run. And froze as the clouds unveiled their proximate salvo, pelting the enormous chamber with a rain of cockroaches.

A sea of rotting fish smacked us then the deck to lie motionless.

Stupefaction wore off when the hell-rain condensed to pure precipitation . . . rinsing the ghastly coat of blood from hair, skin, clothes. We slogged towards the arched portal — feet sliding on insects, birds and fish — and skidded to a standstill as the opening transformed to an opaque murky bulwark.

Wheeling about, I yelled and led my team along the fringe where less bodies were strewn. I had discriminated a crevice across the vault. We were halfway to it, shambling in single-file. The clouds pulsed with tiny dark entities. I could detect a throbbing drone and swiftly, eyes dilating in alarm, motioned for my companions to protect themselves as bees launched at us in a blinding swarm.

Swatting in vain, we had no resort but to race amok, our only thoughts to avoid being stung yet provoking it with our actions. The clouds sank, foggily cloaking the squashy matted layer of death as we floundered upon blood and water and carcasses.

Unconscionably, the gray mist blanketing the floor of the tomb served to regenerate the corpses. Fish seismed, splatting the ground in a rhythmic beat. The limp birds revived to wing, soaring and strafing like bombardiers.

Roaches, never inert, withstanding all but the trample of feet, kept crawling any direction.

The zombie fish, just our luck, were piranha. Hungrily they nipped at our ankles. I kicked them as best I could, arms windmilling at blatting buzzing yellow-and-black kamikazes.

It was an awful experience, yet would not be the ultimate tribulation of that day or night. My ears shunned the splutters and flops, the concussions and crunchings, the inexorable onslaught of bees. Dazed, I persevered through the overkill and carnage, fording to the escape route by instinct. Needing it to be where I found it.

My heaving bosom taut, cheeks striated by cuts, I wrung a dripping beret and whooped to my friends: "This way!"

Remarkably intact, they navigated the bird dives and fish dance, the roach carpet. We tersely met and vacated the gruesome enclave. Only to find ourselves in the cold frosty haze of a blizzard.

None of us were prepared for an arctic snowstorm. Shuddering, squinting against the flakes, the wind's sharkish bite, I chattered that we should trace the contour of the arena so as not to get lost.

It sounded plausible in theory. But there was no perimeter. The blizzard was eternal, a blackhole of whiteness. After taking several strides, we could not even see the gash from which we had emerged.

The five of us linked hands. A chain of reassurance. Rupert now led the way like a bloodhound, unerring in his stalwart willingness to please. He competently guided us to the fissure, or we would never have noticed it with the stinging white obscurity.

I continued quaking long after we eluded that icy wasteland.

Instead of returning to the cockroach-infested
chamber of piranha and attacking birds, we stood on
the hem of a vast ruined forest. Sculptings of partial
trunks and branches. The grotesque agonized shapes
of gnarled skeletons, dark and somber, locked in
pleading stunted poses. Hunched and forlorn,
screeching in silence. A tribe of angular warriors,
paying final homage to their conqueror.

I was fraught by the sordid revelation that we
were staggering through some berserkly shifting maze.
A labyrinth of wind tunnels and storm sewers and
cumulus catacombs, akin to the worst nightmare
of the most demented mind.

A state of hopelessness and depression seized me.
The stone, my earnest mission, seemed unattainable.
I had blundered into an obstruction, which I did not
conceive as related. For my brash recklessness, I would
fail my parents as well as the friends who were trapped
in this puzzlescape beside me.

Setting out to cross the grizzled forest, shivering
and shaken, my spirit downtrodden, I had given up all
hope but for the seed of a sanguine blossom that was
submerged inside. It is every bit as impossible to
completely kill a dream, an aspiration, as it is to
thoroughly abolish love. Always a spark will linger,
however weak and ailing and neglected. And so
I harbored that feeble grain of hope, without my
knowledge; without my consent. It existed.

6

MISSUS DRAGER SCOWLED at the morons she had
been inadvertently thrown in with. She didn't question
the circumstances of how or why she was meandering
through some idiotic mind museum or dream dilemma
that couldn't be a figment since her eyes weren't
shuttered, and couldn't be a mirage when she was
not thirstily meandering through a desert. One thing
she stodgily declined to attribute her present plight
to was that she had been abducted by beings from
outer space because she did not believe in aliens of
any type, shape, size or color. Not even the kind from
another nation, let alone another galaxy!

Minerva (her first name, not Mindy), spuriously
did believe that she was entitled to every advantage and
freebie and privilege available to Mankind by virtue of
being born an American. She was belligerently reluctant
to share her country and its benefits with foreigners,
no matter how many of them might invade like pestilence
across the borders, wash up on shore, or land in a U.F.O.!
That was her opinion and she wasn't going to change it
because a mob of Liberals wanted to turn the country
over to internationals and terrorists.

Not that she cared whether Republicans or
Democrats were in control of the government. They
were all a scandalous lot of swindlers who belonged in
jail. The handshakers and lawmakers were destroying
this country as much as the outsiders!

Her blood pressure was rising, her countenance flushing with venom. She inhaled and exhaled, six breaths in thirty seconds, the breathing exercise she had been taught in her Anger Management Group. She needed to stop thinking about aliens and the unfortunate infuriating fact that her country was being sold out and shanghaied and there wasn't a thing that she or any veritable American could do except argue that Global Warming was a hoax and refuse to vote!

The cadre of clods had become immobile. Sourly Minerva frowned at the number-one tenant she despised, the man who went by "Gord". Perhaps for Gordon. The guy loitered with arms folded, his face assiduously bemused, scrutinizing her and the dummies. She often caught him studying her. Initially the woman was flattered, thinking he admired her handsome features: the square chin; the ski slope of her nose; the fervid rapt glint of her beady eyes. Until she deduced that he was watching *all* his neighbors, surveying them discreetly. Must be a spy! she assumed. He did have the snide swarthy look of a foreigner.

So she started watching *him*. He didn't notice anything unusual, of course; she tended to keep an eye on everybody. You had to these days. She suspected everyone of something, and this guy more than most. He was up to no good, all right. She had even eyeballed him infiltrating latched rooms where he had no business! The armchair sleuth couldn't report him to the police because they probably wouldn't believe a word she said without proof. She had to marshal evidence, then she could expose his plot! Whatever it was.

She surmised he was a member of a cult or terror cell, conspiring to detonate explosive devices. Targeting public monuments, busy structures. She was doing her patriotic duty. Not that she cared about saving lives. Crowded places were as full of people who shouldn't be in the country as the ones who should!

Some days she felt like walking into a restaurant or bank or postal annex with a submachine gun and letting loose some tension! It would make her feel better, and it might clear out some of the riffraff.

Her main purpose for shadowing the man was that she didn't like him.

Not that she liked any of these saps! She sneered at Spiro and Driscoll, who were haggling over which of them should step through an entryway to a vacuous cavern. "Cowards!" Minerva solved the dispute by pushing past the imbeciles.

She was not a person to be easily flabbergasted. What she observed caused her jaw to go slack.

A silvery pear-like vessel hovered. Inexplicably, the seamless craft hung suspended without making a sound or being supported. Minerva, who didn't blink at the phenomalous whirlwind, now wished she had a camera so she could snap a picture and sell it to a tabloid. Her stout conviction that U.F.O. stories were baloney had not been tarnished, but this was a pretty decent fabrication. Oh well. She would try peddling an eyewitness account. That ought to net her a few bucks.

"Wowsers."

"Holy Mother Of Pearl."

Nitwits Driscoll and Spiro were peeking around her like frightened bear cubs.

The third man, Gord, cast a glance at the object as he soberly hoofed by. "Fascinating," he stated. And knocked bare knuckles against the hull. His voice echoed from the other side: "You're not afraid, are you?"

"Go dry up!" Minerva retorted. And strutted by as if it were nothing special.

The timid twins scampered close behind.

Missus Drager heard a snarl. Swinging about, she gaped at a nine-foot heathen.

The Alien

The creature's bifurcated head, a protuberant eye-bulb at the summit of each segment, bobbed on a retracting neck. Its mouth, with bayonets for teeth, formed an unsavory aperture in a burly abdomen. Three deuces of limbs equipped with lethal dinosaur talons, the sub-set for speed and agility, extended from a ridged torso. Minerva's eyes scanned the ugly-buggly, took in its lurid nature. "You must be one of those monsters they're always searching for on T.V.," was her assessment.

The pair of dunces quivered as they, too, rotated towards the behemoth. For males, they shrieked like schoolgirls.

"Jeez, what sissies!" Minerva scorned. "Didn't you never have monsters under your beds when you were kids? What's the big deal?"

"Duck!" a masculine timbre exhorted.

"Nope, I think it's a chupacabra," declared Minerva.

"I meant, get down!" Gord decreed.

Minerva turned, saw he was training a handgun at her chest, and starchily acquiesced. "Why didn't you say so?" She scooted out of the line of fire.

The goobers pivoted to find a gun barrel unsteadily directed at them. Yipping, they threw themselves aside.

The weapon discharged. The creature, for all its ominous hulking grandeur, was annihilated with one lousy bullet. The thing's belly blew up.

Missus Drager was underwhelmed. She was also enraged, splashed by a wave of gobbled gook. *"Ewwww!"*

Minerva fumed to herself that she'd like to maim and mutilate that insipid girl with the beret for leaving her door ajar during her aunt's visit, which made it impossible not to eavesdrop and overhear something about a lost gem. Anyone listening at their own door couldn't help but be enticed to trail the girl, could they?

Wiping gore from her cheeks, she tisked at the muck on her sweater. It was her best cardigan. She shook her head. What was the world coming to?

7

THE FOREST OF DOOM was one of the most miserable
sites I have ever seen. If you think about it, the woods
are so alive and green — burgeoning with wildlife and
foliage; germinating, adding more rings, producing more
generations to the scheme of things. Even the white
dormant mantle of Winter abides the auspice of Spring.
But on that derelict plain I saw no growth; I heard no
symphony of birds or patter of beasts. It was silent and
barren, the life drained out, and no promise remained.

     My own mood was as desolate, or so I thought.
We think when we are morose that this is as empty as
we can feel, that our pain is as dismal as any. There are
levels to emotion. We are never as bereft as the aftermath
of a forest so devastated, so debilitated, that there is no
hope of renewal — not now, not ever.

     The human spirit transcends that rock-bottom
degree, though our angst might block us from the
discovery that it is not the end. One way or another,
we will go on. Often we have to survive insurmountable
odds just enough to weather the storm, to get through
the darkness that precedes the sunrise. There is
something amazingly restorative in those early rays
of light.

     "What is this place?" queried Rhonda, gulping.

     "It is Noplace," answered Juniper. "And dat is
someplace, but no place you want to be."

     As if in condolence, the very air itself had dwindled
to a paucitude. Our lips flapped like guppies striving to
breathe.

   To illustrate how profoundly tragic was this terrain,
the soil itself seemed to cringe beneath our respectful
treads, as if it had exceeded so far beyond its limit that
it now could not bear the slightest touch, the gentlest
footfall.

   "What do you think caused it?" asked Terence in
Rupert's non-canine tone; in a rare instance when he
forgot to be a dog.

   Rupert dashed to sniff a burned statue, then
galumphed to the shelter of the group.

   "Nothing good," Tonka intoned. "And that's all
we need to know."

   I was quiet, too disconsolate to share my feelings.
We trudged onward, the smell of scorched bark bedeviling
our nostrils, polluting our lungs. The suffocating weight
of countless tortured ghosts bore upon me. I faltered,
panicking. It felt that my brittle bones would fracture
under a metaphoric boulder.

   It was that moment when the sky, a dusky coalish
hue, flickered yellow and orange. Streaks of electric heat
dazzled down, igniting black tips of already dessicated
stalks. Voltage leaped in blue or red veins, zapping the
truncated boughs, dancing along amputated appendages
of these sylvan soldiers.

   We reacted, fleeing the firestorm's hostility. Irate
clouds, jagged arrows followed us. Booms and crackles
resonated, while spears of flame sliced air to ribbons.
Javelins struck the smoldered bones of huddled guards,
protecting us in their petrified throes.

   "Were you a storm chaser?" I inquired, puffing
beside Tonka, although we were actually the ones being
chased.

   His response was a garbled cry. As we ran amidst
the tree-men, bolts of intensity sizzled the ground,
disseminating a blue net of energy over the traumatized
mead. We had to hop to avoid our tootsies being toasted.

The field of wattage subsided. Dirt began to froth, spitting clumps. Tree stubs came alive, acrimoniously flexent, and unrooted to stampede. Boldly Tonka lured the lumbering herd, gesticulating with his arms, laughing and jigging, taunting the stumps then sprinting away.

"Were you a rodeo clown?" I shouted after him.

A distant wail: *"Can't say that I was!"*

He led the trees round and round, till their charges of current expired. They toppled like logs.

Decadent corpses, the exhumed bones of animals rose out of the earth, lunging upright with terrible volition. Mottled decrepit reptiles and mammals; ivory incarnations. Their fetid presence was sufficiently unnerving. The fiends scuttled toward us.

An undead owl swooped, peeling the soggy beret off my belfry. "Hey!" I hollered, and swerved to lope after.

While I was pursuing the hat-snatcher, my friends had their hands full, fending off stinky carcasses or stick animals. I could only catch glimmers. Juniper engaged in a wrestling match with a beaver, embracing the moldy thrashing critter. Rhonda booting skellies, jumping over lizards and rodents, being chased by a skunk. Rupert hounded by the bones of wolves.

A born-again bear sparred with Tonka, circling and boxing. They grappled and rolled.

"Were you a bear trainer?" I questioned in passing.

"Doubtful. I'm not very good!"

Ground ruptured and split as a gigantic skeleton clambered out. An immense dinosaur shirked soil and reared above the transplanted tract. Zigzags of lightning licked the regal Rex. This lord of raptors craned his skull, then plucked the bear between grinning jaws. He mashed the morsel.

Capitulating my beret, I hauled Tonka to his feet. He grabbed his brim from the tyrant's path. We rushed before the stomping brute.

Sweeping dust off his hat to seat it on his head, Tonka was astonished when it expanded into a stovepipe. Even more astonished when he pulled a black wand out of the crown. The dowel elongated as it was extracted.

"A magician!" I jubilously proclaimed, my legs pumping as fast as my heart.

"Could be!" the man concurred, donning the hat and holding the brim with one hand, the wand with his other. The baton acted as a lightning rod and attracted a sparkle. "Oh!" He nearly dropped the stick in consternation. Then cleverly diverted the flow of electricity past his shoulder.

The rampaging bone-monster's joints, tethered by ligaments of static, were scattered like bowling pins and the dinosaur minimized to a pile of clanking parts.

"Over here!" Juniper, Rhonda and Rupert beckoned us to an exit. Wherever it led, the hollow or enclosure couldn't be worse than this offensive lightning socket!

We had almost reached them when a hefty sonic boom rumbled and a bright oblique strobe of juice lanced Tonka. He was encased by hot blue malice and rigidly jolted. There was nothing I could do but watch mortified as his body spasmed incessantly . . . then was released.

Tonka fell. It seemed to take forever, though it was only a long heartbeat.

8

SPIRO VISCOTTI'S FAVORITE PASTIME was lobbing triangles of pizza at the wall and seeing how long they would adhere. That was as much fun as driving through a red light, but less of an adrenaline high. And he could get busted. For the driving thing, not the pizza. Unless it was somebody else's wall. Like his mother's. She said he was a criminal and called the cops. Who wouldn't have arrested him but it was his third complaint and they wanted to teach him a lesson. The judge didn't like the looks of him so he did two months for vandalism, even though the alleged "damage" could be washed off. His mother claimed the tomato sauce left a permanent stain. He filled her Jacuzzi with tomato sauce. It took a lot of cans. Then she said he was nuts and should be committed.

The crud on his dingy white teeshirt from landing in the body pit reminded him of that tomato sauce. It probably wouldn't wash out. The liquid that spurted from the punctured alien lifeform — or pollutant mutant, whichever — had corroded teeny holes into the cotton that for sure weren't coming out. It pricked like a cactus tine where the goop contacted skin, but what was he gonna do, call the cops to arrest an alien? Or maybe he should sue the guy with the gun! And call the men in the white jackets for this witch-broad and the dude with no eyebrows!

Okay, so maybe his attitude needed adjustment like the shrink his ma sent him to wrote on a tablet.

Spiro glommed the notebook to read what the scumbag was scribbling about him. The doctor had plenty of wisdom for examining people's brains, but he didn't have too many brains for how to handle somebody's fist.

Spiro just wanted to know what the wack-job meant by the crack about living with his mother. And being afraid of elves. Dwarfs too. Little people were scary! He still couldn't watch *The Wizard Of Oz*. It gave him nightmares.

Lotsa grown men had phobias. There was no need to label him with funny terms like Pupaphobic! Who wouldn't be afraid of puppets? Who didn't dread dolls and children and the moonrise? So clocks made him antsy! It wasn't so weird. And "supercilious" — what the heck was that supposed to mean?

The loudmouth jackhammer got what he deserved for calling Spiro names and blabbing to his mother what they talked about. It was like confessing to a priest. It didn't matter what you said. You could spill your intestines, purge your soul and walk away scot-free, absolved of sin, your conscience lighter. The doc had an obligation. Those sessions were confidential. Now his ma knew everything. All of his inner workings and foibles. The deepest fears; his darkest deeds; ammunition to use against him. And that doctor was missing a few teeth.

Spiro smirked with satisfaction, massaging his right fist with his left palm. He wasn't sorry. Nor was he bothered by the extraordinary situation he had bumbled into: rambling the bowels of a freak zone accompanied by these losers. He was in it for the treasure. He wasn't about to let *them* rob the girl of her inheritance without dividing the spoils with him! They could do the hard stuff; he would be there to collect the prize. Only, for him nothing was ever a cinch.

Old Lady Drager (she had to be at least fifty)
reeked of flowers, one of his anxieties. Anthrophobia.
Then there was the fear of beards, Pogo-No-Phobia.
He had foregone his afternoon shave, and his face
was developing stubble!

Spiro's armpits were lathered in sweat. His heart
palpitated, banging to get out. He strained to disguise
his malaise with a shellac of composure, coaching
himself to breathe, to rein in the galloping tension.

Another challenge was his fear of going insane.
It was like the insomnia, exacerbated by worrying
that he couldn't go to sleep. Once you were afraid
of something, the terror could snowball and lead to
other fears, until you were even afraid of being afraid:
Phobophobia!

Hands clenched, Spiro eyed Wunderbar — envious
that Driscoll was too asinine to be concerned. The dope
usually wore a creepy smile, like he was exorbitantly
pleased with himself. Nobody should be *that* pleased!

As for the other man, he always looked bleak and
meditative. Spiro was afraid of him too. The guy didn't
seem afraid of anything, which made him irregular.
Everyone in their right mind is afraid of something.
Spiro suspected the guy *wasn't* in his right mind.
Or else he was a crook. A jewel thief. Maybe a burglar.
He was always sneaking around.

Perhaps a mad scientist, conducting arcane
experiments on his neighbors!

Spiro had dreams that he was strapped to
a table, being tinkered with in his sleep, but that could
just be aliens. He wasn't afraid of Little Green Men,
only little people who weren't green. Or gray. And elves;
he hated elves.

His doctor had dubbed this qualm Lilliphobia
after Lilliput from *Gulliver's Travels*, and branded him
a "case study" like he should be under a microscope.
More reasons to punch the twerp's lights out.

Spiro was a paradox (another name), according to the shrink. His aversions were irrational. He wasn't afraid of the things he *should* fear, as a rule. Though he had been a bit bent out of shape over that six-legged sucker. Maybe he was cured!

The four unfriends had scaled a plateau. Spiro's eyes registered a patch of whopping speckled and solid fungus, knobbed or umbrella-capped, sprouting along the shade between two oblong formations connected by an array of plumbing-like conduits with what appeared to be smokestacks at the top. The impression sank in.

His eyes bulged. Lips quavered. His tongue felt swollen. "M-m-m-mushrooms!" he stuttered, complexion paling.

Driscoll scoffed, "What's wrong? You aren't scared of them, are you?"

Spiro struggled to keep calm. "Of course not, that would be crazy," the neurotic denied.

To his repulsion, a batch of the toadstools moved. *They have feet!* He clapped a hand over his yap to smother a scream.

"Looks like termite mountains," the biddy opined.

"Or some manner of power apparatus," hypothesized the mystery gun-toting thief.

"Do we look like termites to you?" a tiny voice protested.

"Little people!" To Spiro's dismay, four-inch folk had tromped from an opening at the base of one tower. They were dressed in beige-gray coveralls out of a fabric approximating the texture of a toadstool.

The walking mushrooms were dropped, revealing more of the lilliputian gnomes.

"It's — it's — Leprechauns!" stammered Spiro, cheeks scarlet, ready to have conniptions.

The spokesperson, a bossy miniature as acerbic as Missus Drager, holding a cone to her mouth refuted: "Do we look Irish to you? We're Dervish, from Dervy! You might say we're Hill People, except that we live in mounds, which are more like ant-hills only bigger!" She gestured at a village of dome-like dwellings on a bluff. The homes were about the circumference of Hula Hoops. "That's Dervy! We're a rascally race, like the Little People of Sweden called Vittror. Except we aren't Swedish, we're Dervish! And we're probably not as tall as them either."

"Well, I guess that makes us giants," growled Missus Drager in a threatening tone. "I've often wished I were big enough to step on everybody else!" She tilted her head back and laughed raucously.

Yet had sounded wistful, Spiro diametrically impugned.

Driscoll sniggered.

The smallish clan stared up with abhorrence. Then milled in a frenetic hubbub, shrilling as if a single voice: "Eeeeeeeeeeeeeeeeeeeeeeeeek!!!"

"Oh gosh, I think I frightened them!" Another braying chortle.

Driscoll and Drager, even the thief had no difficulty accepting the existence of these pipsqueaks. They weren't terrified of the shorties, whereas Spiro was on the verge of a major meltdown. An eye had a tic. His stomach hurt. His throat was in a vise. He felt certain this had to be a prank. Someone was goading him again — needling him like a voodoo doll. It happened all the time. One of his neighbors, one of these three, must be the punkster. That's why they weren't surprised.

He'd show them! He wasn't going to give whoever it was the gratification of seeing him go ballistic. Standing on one leg, raising an arm perpendicular at the elbow, Spiro ad-libbed a simulated yoga pose. He could do this, he told himself. He just needed to find his center.

The three potential culprits goggled at him like he had acquired a spare head. Above the first. Sure, *this* they thought was weird — not the runts, or any of the rest of this far-fetched Wizard-Of-Odd hullabaloo!

The impudent imps were also gandering him. As if they weren't perfectly peculiar!

Spiro paid his spectators no heed. Let them gawk. He was going to stay placid no matter what.

His leg got tired. How did flamingos do it? He had to lapse to a normal position.

Meanwhile, the pixies went back to doing whatever they were doing inside the mountains. If there was a sun in the interior of this midworld, the towers would have been erected East and West so the shadow was constant between them for much of the day.

Several of the wee folk emerged from one tor pushing wheelbarrows, on which they each loaded a mushroom that had been added to the heap. They promptly trundled their harvest into the plant, entering a door in the opposite alp.

A noisy mechanism commenced grinding and whirring. The pipes linking the minarets vibrated. Smokestacks billowed with noxious black smog. The four humans had to clamp their nostrils shut at the vile odor that poured out.

Spiro's eyes stung, the air had become so polluted. The toadstools must be toxic. He was just as afraid of the ones you could eat.

The Drager dame groused that they ought to continue trailing the girl.

Wunderbunder agreed. Spiro himself was more than eager to leave this nightmare of mushrooms and itsies behind. He pretended that he didn't care, grudgingly assented. The thief or sulky mad scientist fanned his face and nodded.

It wasn't that they valued the opinions of the others. But when you're lost, whether you know you're lost or not, in a perturbantly unfamiliar landscape . . . it's better not to be alone. Even if those you are not alone with are the very people you would ordinarily be the gladdest to get away from!

As the titans were about to shuffle off — their female associate grumbling that the midgekins were lucky she didn't wanna muss a good pair of shoes — the industrial facility clanged a strident signal, its duo cores overheating from a jammed toadstool was Spiro's estimation. The towers swayed. A roiling sea of carbon expelled. The structures tremored as if they were rockets poised to launch. Like nuclear reactors, the energy plant's peaks erupted and spewed a dose of gases that ascended to paint a mushroom cloud below the ceiling.

Spiro tittered with glee. "That's what they get for using poison as fuel," he blithely pronounced. Any insane risk was bound to blow up sooner or later. It was the nature of folly. Not that he was wiser. He was simply more afraid.

He cowered at the tide of "idgets" (as he anointed them) evacuating the structures.

The tiny laborers, beholding the dark cloud above, emitted a unison gasp of awe.

These mushroom worshippers fell to their knees in exaltation, and bowed with reverence to the effigy of their god.

"They believe," described the jewel-thief gunman.

What they believed — that the disaster was meant to be; that the visitors brought bad luck; that it was a sign the world would end — was of less consequence.

Four incorrigible gargantuans, lacking faith, regarded the scene in addled appraisal. Then tramped forth after their own passions and devotions.

9

INCONSOLABLY I KNELT by Tonka, whose lifeless body still lay on the desecrated forest floor. I sobbed over a man I knew naught about, except the most important things — that he was noble, generous, and nice. That he was a true friend.

It was all I needed to know at a time like this. The rest of who we were did not determine whether we were loved or how much; whether we would be missed by those who really knew us when we were gone. The rest might inspire others not as near, even strangers, to acknowledge our demise. Possibly, if we left an indelible mark, to honor the date.

I didn't know if Tonka left a mark for strangers to remember. I did not even know his original name. All that mattered then, at that moment, was that I knew the man. After innumerable exchanges about what he had been in the past, I came to appreciate that who he was now in his heart, and who he had been to me, were what counted in the end.

Sometimes we don't get a chance to say goodbye, to adequately tell someone how much we care. We can only hope they knew from what was shared in casual days with no end in sight. Did we give of ourselves enough? Were we truly there, fathoming every detail?

Juniper, Rhonda, and Rupert knelt with me. Around us was quiet. Once we stopped worrying about the lightning, the electricity and eerie commotion had faded, leaving only the smell of ash and sorrow in the air.

There were no words, but we tried to speak.

"Dat's it den," Juniper sighed. "He was a good man."

"The best," Ronnie affirmed.

"A pal," Terence imparted.

"He was a magic man," I stated. For the record.

I had laid his wand and black silk hat on his torso. Our heads drooped, burdened by grief. The stick rolled. My head jerked up. I trained damp eyes upon his chest, his hat. He breathed! *"Ahhh!"* I could not believe it, for there was no pulse, no indication of life. And yet he drew breath!

Tonka sat up. The hat cascaded. In a French accent he professed: "I remember!"

The words we had awaited. Somehow they were not as grand as I expected. I don't mean *what* he remembered. Just the fact that he did.

For the man I had come to know, with his riddles and constraints, was already complete to me. I suddenly feared losing him, a second time, even as I regained his friendship.

I know that sounds rather selfish. But I liked him as he was. Would I like him equally if he were somebody else? It was a quandary. If I was his friend, I should want him to be happy. I should want him to feel undiminished, even if that meant he was no longer the man I knew.

I could see that Juniper and Rhonda were feeling a bit daunted by the news. Terence was back to being Rupert and not thinking too much.

Tonka — even his name would be different, I realized — smiled sadly, sharing our uncertainty and misgivings.

But it was inevitable, for life is an unrelenting chain of events.

One thing leads us to another, then brings us
to another and so on, with a panoply of interlocking
elements. So many pieces that are connected, falling
into place exactly, because of what preceded. Because
of what needed to transpire. And sometimes because
of what didn't.

Our dear friend was back with us by miracle,
by design, because he had more to share with us.
We five were precisely where we were destined to be
at this juncture in Space and Time. That is all I can
tell you. Fate is like that. Very precise. Very mystical.
Very incontrovertible. Some things are meant to be.

But at times there seems no purpose. No justice
in what is done or received, in what is dished out.
You have to look extremely hard to find the good lying
beyond or behind the bad. My life story seemed that
way, until I made some worthy friends . . . who had
harrowing yet thrilling tales of their own.

The five of us roved on, blissful to be reunited,
as Tonka related a spellbinding history.

And solved the conundrum of his birth:
"My name was Armond Arno Benoit, which was like
having t'ree first names. Most people, including my
fazer, referred to me by all of zem at once. Mozer
called me Arno. My family lived in a quaint hamlet,
Mont Charmante. Ze factory Fazer worked in went
bankrupt. It was a harsh Winter and we couldn't
afford heat. Ze baby died. My parents were so
distraught by ze pressures, ze loss of a child, zey too
were stricken. I tried to care for zem at ze age of eight,
but my efforts failed. Ze loving family I had known was
gone. Zere were no kinfolks who could feed an extra
mout'. I was sent to an orphanage wit' nozing to my
name."

He told us the institution was operated by
a charity that depended on donations. Without its
factory, his town could not survive.

People exodused to cities, their properties abandoned. The children's home was closed and boarded as well, the waifs dispersed. Arno was taken to Paris, but no orphanage had room for him and he wound up on the street.

Padding barefoot to a park, he watched a beggar named Marcel perform amateurish tricks. Arno was enthralled and tagged after the man, who covertly lived in the cellar of an old woman's house. Marcel tried to dissuade the boy but, like a pup starved for food and affection, Arno dogged his every step until the beggar grew accustomed to him.

The man did his stunts and the kid held his hand out for coins. In the alley by a nightclub, Arno found a black top-hat. Marcel enthusiastically incorporated the chapeau as a prop. Arno joined the act and the tricks improved. Their audiences increased from stragglers to modest crowds. The pair solicited money in the hat as their patrons applauded.

Then the old lady whose basement they occupied passed away. Her house was sold, and the squatters had nowhere to sleep.

Two sisters, Etta and Metta, compensated Marcel an ample sum for Arno. The beggar wanted him to have a bed, warm meals, a family. The friends parted ways.

Arno cried for weeks. The sisters needed an errand boy to do everything they had no time for. Which was everything. They were lazy and rotund, while he was too scrawny. They scroogily fed and often whipped him for things their sibling had done. He ran away, combing les rues for Marcel. The beggar could not be located. He was touring the province with a small circus, Arno would eventually learn.

The boy espied a black top-hat, gusted off a gent's head by the wind. He chased the hat in hopes it belonged to his friend. Prospecting the satin lining, he was disappointed to find a different maker's label.

The hat's owner caught up with him. Instead of a reward, noticing the child's unkempt clothing and hair, the gangly man offered him a job and a home. "A useful lad like yourself might be, well, useful," grinned Monsieur Envoler (which meant to vanish into thin air).

Roland Envoler was a wealthy but private fellow who retained no servants. The aristocrat had no need of menial laborers for he was a sorcerer. Anything he wished could be attained with the stroke of a wand, the mixing of a potion, reciting some magic words.

Arno was hired primarily out of pity. His tasks were dull, superfluous, more to keep him busy than to aid his employer. Bored, he begged Roland to make him an apprentice. Monsieur Envoler refused. Wizards had become sparse since the days of witch-hunts and inquisitions. The magus had mentored someone years ago who quit in the middle of his training then stole the book of incantations. This traitor lived lavishly and violated the code of discretion by demonstrating magic in public, flaunting it to settle scores. He was arrested as a public nuisance, for cheating and profiteering. The turncoat turned in Roland, his benefactor, who bribed officials not to charge *him*.

Monsieur Envoler told Arno he would never entrust his secrets to anyone else. The boy, however, had absorbed a few things by merely watching.

Gaspard was released from jail. Penniless, divested of the spellbook, he attempted to purloin the sorcerer's wand late one night. As a gale assaulted windowpanes, the men fought over the precious implement.

Arno awoke to find the mansion burning. He rushed to save Roland in his bedchamber and beheld a battle. Gaspard gripped the wand, but a saber protruded from one leg, and a fireplace poker had pierced a shoulder. A laceration oozed down the side of his face.

Relying on the charms he knew by heart, the ingredients at hand, Roland resisted by conjuring flameballs and lasers, hurling objects from around him. He was in worse condition than his opponent. Blood gushed from a mortal wound in his chest.

The final volley: daggers from a wall display, impaling Gaspard's arms, knocking the wand out of his fist. Arno secured the stick. The man fled with what life and dignity were left.

Roland collapsed. Arno helped him to his bed and there he died, after whispering to protect the rod from Gaspard. "I will," Arno promised.

He was alone in the world again at age eleven, his sole possession a wizard's wand that he did not know how to wield.

Arno sought again the beggar Marcel. When the circus went out of business, the man had returned to his old streets and habits. He welcomed the boy, overjoyed to see him. Arno confided that he was the guardian of a magical source. Marcel thought he was joking. "Fine, boy, you are a wizard and I am a genuine magician! We should get lots of francs with that angle!" he wheezed.

"I'm serious, Marcel. I do not know how to use it, but I do have a sorcerer's wand," Arno insisted.

Marcel discerned that he was being truthful. "Then, my boy, we shall be rich!" he cheered.

Arno explained that the wand had enormous power, that they couldn't risk attention. Gaspard might be lurking, or the police might take them into custody!

"Don't worry! Nobody needs to know that our illusions are real," assuaged Marcel. "We'll be pretending to be magicians. And we'll be famous, for giving the people more than they bargain for! The best part — they won't be able to figure out how we are doing it."

Man and boy traveled out of the city, hiking, hitching rides. In a deserted pasture Marcel instructed Arno to practice, but not a thing resulted when the boy waved the wand.

"You aren't doing it right," Marcel critiqued. "Tap the air!"

He next advised, "Trace a circle!"

Then snapped his fingers bleating "I know, I know!" and recommended to point the baton authoritatively and emote, "Abracadabra!"

None of this did the trick.

Arno addressed the rod, which was humble and dark — a length of wood neither smooth nor rugged, although its texture evoked patterns and whorls, undulations in the mind. "Listen, maybe you and I should get acquainted," he murmured, holding the shaft like a sword in front of his eyes. "I'm not your enemy. And I don't mean to hurt anyone. But this is really embarrassing. I told my friend you're magical, and he's not going to believe me unless you give him a sample. Please do something. Anything. For my sake. I'd be very grateful."

The boy laughed aloud as the wand surged with tactile and audible resonance, like a kitten's purr.

Aiming the dowel before him, he focused on the image of a dove in his brain. With a poof, a white possum was snuffling the grass.

"Okay . . ." He gave it another go, envisioning a goose. What he got was a white rabbit. "Eh! All right!" At least they could use the bunny in their act. Maybe the possum too.

The stick had a sense of humor. Arno thought of a penguin (he'd always wanted one for a pet), and produced a goldfish swimming in a glass of water. "Closer!" he kudoed. A spider monkey (another cool pet) was substituted by a skunk. "Ohhh!"

The Magician

The fickle wand would not cooperate, try as the lad did.

Marcel shrugged. "It's still impressive!" he declared.

They gathered the rabbit, possum, and goldfish — plus a toaster, military boot, soccer ball, artist easel, and stuffed panda — but not the skunk, and headed back to Paris.

They were swiftly raking in francs and could rent an apartment. Marcel purchased tuxedos with tails and bow-ties. He wore a black beret, while Arno donned the top-hat. Auditioning at a club, they were billed as The Marvelous Marcel and Amazing Armond.

No prestidigious sleight went as intended, but the audience loved the comedic unpredictable nature of what would materialize and what was announced. They were a hit.

With popularity came exposure, which led to their posters being plastered all over the city. An angry crippled sorcerer descried a familiar face: the kid who was with Envoler the night he died.

Gaspard visited Club Monstrueux to see for himself. Sure enough, the boy had the wand, but his skills were inferior to Gaspard's. The dastardly apprentice vowed to avenge his limp and his impoverished stature. He would take the wizard's wand and become Gaspard The Great. No, Gaspard The Grand. He would have the greatest act on Earth! Maybe Gaspard The Great would fit better, he decided. No, he would have the *grandest* act on Earth! So what if he never completed the training; he didn't need a bunch of spells and potions. Once he had the wand, he could do whatever he pleased. The charlatan cackled in the flickering light of his tacky hotel room.

What he didn't know was that the magicians would embark the next morning to America for five months of shows with a theatrical revue. They were the headliners. Arno's mother had taught him English. They were even scheduled for some gigs on T.V.

Gaspard arrived too late. Their ship had sailed.
Their star was rising. It made him furious. The luckless
apprentice smuggled himself aboard a ship, hiding in the
cargo-hold with the rats. He had always wanted to take
a cruise.

The stowaway was seasick his entire maiden voyage.

New York City was the troupe's first booking.
Gaspard ambushed the pair after they stepped through
the stage exit, trailing them with a butcher knife under
his coat. He brandished the blade and accosted them
beside an alley, forcing them away from the sidewalk to
a dead-end against a brick wall.

"Give it to me!" the pathetic man hissed.

Recognizing Gaspard's face vividly from his
nightmares, Arno withdrew the wand out of his jacket.

"No funny business!" the robber warned. "Hand
it over slowly, the tip towards you!"

Arno complied, the stick throbbing as he
surrendered it. Marcel began to weep. They would
lose everything!

"Shut up, you sniveling old fart!" rebuked
Gaspard. He scowled at Arno. "I can't let you live.
You'd keep trying to take it away, wouldn't you?"

Marcel shouted, "It doesn't belong to you!"
And reached desperately for the wand.

The knife plunged into his abdomen. He sank
to his knees.

Arno screamed and clutched his friend.

Gaspard, backing up to flee, directed the baton
at them and muttered one of the few spells he recalled:
"Endus horrendous, lightning frightening. Gone is your
life, as will all be rightening!" The stick didn't work for
him unless he chanted magic words.

The wand buckled. Frowning, Gaspard repeated
the rhyme. The staff ejected a stream of electricity,
enveloping the boy and Marcel. Both convulsed in
agony.

Simultaneously, the voltage bounced off the wall and ricocheted to Gaspard. He shrieked like a dying man. The wand fell from his hand, breaking the circuit, shrinking in size.

Arno slumped with Marcel to the pavement, a silk chapeau crushed beneath him.

A boy would rouse from a fugue not knowing his name. He would find two dead bodies and not know them either.

Numbly picking up a folded hat, a curious stick, he tucked the rod inside the brim's crown and drifted from the alley, merging into a crowd of pedestrians. He didn't know that he spoke French or was French. He forgot he had a French accent. All he knew was that he had a hat. So he put it on his head.

When the people who netted him like an alley stray, delivering him to another institution, asked for his name — he told them the only moniker that he could elicit, the logo on his favorite yellow dump-truck: Tonka.

10

DRISCOLL WUNDERBAR LIKED CHICKS. Not the kind
that wore skirts; not the ones who giggled a lot and
painted their lips. He liked fuzzy yellow baby chicks.
They were peachy to play with, so delicate and cute,
like pitching a kitten at a little kid. The child got clawed
or the kitty got roughed up. It was amusing to watch.

He additionally liked to torment his neighbors.
He especially liked to strategically liberate a chick to
toddle through Spiro Viscotti's door. The guy left it
open a bit, paranoid his room might run out of oxygen.
When he noticed the bird, he would race down the
corridor keening. The maintenance man would have
to clear it away. Spiro was chicken of chickens.
That never failed to make Driscoll guffaw.

But then, he relished a multitude of wondrous
things. Quirky fare that others wouldn't pay attention
to, or might think deranged.

There was, of course, the game of testing to see
what agitated Spiro. That was often good for a chuckle.
Even music caused alarm! Drisk would hum and whistle
outside the man's doorway, or blast the radio with his
portal wide. He once "borrowed" as many cordless clocks
as he could, slinking like a phantom through the building,
and mischievously arranged the tickers like time-bombs
inside Spiro's residence — to greet his return.

The fruition of the tactic was stupendous!
The poor man mutely tossed a box of donuts and
carton of milk then howled for the hills.

More specifically, the outdoors. He climbed a tree, although the guy was a raving Dendrophobe and afraid of those too, and wouldn't come out of it for seventeen hours. The Fire Department had to be summoned but couldn't pry him loose! They finally had to chop off the limb to which he clung.

Yes, getting Spiro's goat was quite a pleasure.

Other hobbies included licking postage stamps, even the peel-off type (he savored the flavor). Constructing model bridges out of used ear swabs stuck together by the wax (a fairly slow process which necessitated a great deal of patience). Filling a toothpaste tube with carpenter glue. Writing cryptic messages in blood on mirrors and walls. Concealing things so people couldn't find them; things they kept in a regular spot or were utilizing a moment ago — it drove them nuts looking and looking around, scratching their heads, wondering how the thing could've just disappeared or walked away!

It was very interesting to orchestrate havoc with some minor transgression, like spilling baby oil to grease a floor; removing most of the screws from tables and chairs (wheelchairs were hilarious); emancipating a wicked-seeming spider in a woman's hair; hanging a rat by its tail in a shower stall. Deceased birds and rodents and snakes were nifty for sliding under the covers or pillow on someone's bed, or placing in a public toilet. And dismembered parts had ways of showing up in the strangest places: cupboards, drawers, shoes, pockets; those plastic containers of food in the fridge.

Animals were fun, but far more he enjoyed toying with humans. They had such a prolific gamut of emotions and expressions!

Driscoll's pet peeve and proclivity at the same time was children. He wasn't afraid of them like Viscotti. They revolted him, gave him goosebumps out of repugnance, as well as for the titillation of bullying them. Oh, he loved to make them cry, to see their faces pucker. But he didn't steal their candy. No, he would give them candy, lure them with sweets into a baited trap. He wasn't a pervert. He wished to leave *visible* scars — embossing their arms and legs with his teeth; etching diagrams and doodles in their soles and palms with a scalpel; prickling their flesh with red-hot knitting needles.

But on Halloween, instead of candy, Driscoll had passed out maggots and worms.

He liked to pull their hair strand by strand. Hide in their closet at night and nudge the door ajar inch by inch, or recline under their bed and shake the mattress; tell them he was the boogeyman then slip away while they ran bawling to Mommy and Daddy . . . a harmless diversion.

Driscoll was ashamed he had lost his equanimity with the alien. Despite his macabre propensities, he didn't handle unexpected things so well. And that thing was huge! He wasn't a wimp like Spiro, but occasionally something did disturb even him.

He liked praying mantids. Sometimes he captured the mantises to inspect, then he would eat them. They were crunchy. Driscoll considered himself a *preying* mantid. But he wouldn't want to meet one that was a dozen feet tall. That would freak him out too!

His impetus for aligning with this rabble brigade was that he liked to meddle. He didn't care about the gem they were after, except to deprive them of getting their greedy paws upon it. He liked to be contrary.

Scoundrel was his middle name.

It was his father's idea. The man reasoned that with a first name like Driscoll and a last name like Wunderbar, his son would need a tough middle name to not get picked on.

Driscoll took the term to heart and was never bullied. He didn't give the bullies a chance. He got them before they could even think about getting him. By adolescence, he had a reputation for being weird and they were all afraid of him. They ran when they saw his pudgy pallid face and skinhead coming. (He had shaved his scalp since age five.)

Crepuscular should have been his middle name. He liked being nocturnal and rarely slept. In the darkness he felt sleek and cunning, a consummate predator.

His parents were the opposite of aberrant. His family had been a picture-perfect Norman Rockwell portrait. No siblings or pets in the frame. His parents were too frightened to spawn more of his kind. Also, to bring animals or a normal baby home.

Driscoll's piggish eyes flitted snarkily at the trio of dolts he was mimicking and reviling. To his exquisite mirth, not one of them had the least notion of who he was or what he was capable of, and nobody ever did. Not his parents or teachers or counselors. Certainly not his friends. He had none. He was always a loner and liked being a pariah, liked being feared. It made him feel strong, because he wasn't hindered by concepts of propriety.

The man vaingloriously perceived he was a singular individual, shrift of society's cramping etiquette and formalities. An immoral breed of his own. He didn't go around spouting this philosophy, however. How could he? It was his little secret.

Smirking, reveling in debauched mockery, Driscoll cleared his esophagus with exaggerated ceremony. "I think we are no longer following the girl," he proposed. "We've turned so many corners, she could be anywhere. She might even be following us!"

"You're probably right," grumped Missus Drager.

"I bet there *is* no jewel," pouted Spiro.

"And no way out of here!" Driscoll incited.

"These walls look like they're made of wind. We could probably step through them. And there is so a jewel. There has to be!" rasped Missus Drager.

"Yeah," Spiro nodded.

"You don't know that," disparaged Driscoll.

"I heard it," Missus Drager coarsed. "I wouldn't be here if I didn't!"

"Wherever here is," mumbled Spiro.

"Think what you want. You're both deluded. We might be in a dream for all you know." Driscoll didn't believe that. He was messing with them.

The fourth member of the party was idly stretching his arm through a wall.

An echo arose.

"Now, what from Hell is that?" Missus Drager sniped.

A cadence of feet pounded, yet the floors of the windworld appeared as nebulous as the walls.

A corps of juveniles traipsed into view, to the shock of Spiro *and* Driscoll. Even Missus Drager was aghast. The kids were like mangled dolls — with blackened eyes, bruised chins, gaps in their toothy smiles; arms erratically awry, and legs that bent where there was no joint.

But the other guy, the man who made Driscoll a tad uneasy with his coy gazes and prowlings, was unfazed.

From the rear flocked a bevy of fluffy forest critters: moles and voles, badgers, otters, bear cubs and fawns. Smoke wisped from blackened pelts. Behind them hobbled ranks of urban creatures: cats and dogs, pigeons and rabbits, mauled and marred.

The four adults were surrounded by abused children, whose visages might be cherubic yet their teeth were sharp and their eyes ferocious. No longer innocent lambs, they were warped souls damned by becoming the same as their oppressors.

Animals, killed by human negligence or cruelty, flanked the kids — abiding turns once the children finished meting punishment upon the scapegoats. Each would be held responsible for enacting the abuse or tolerating it in their home, their neighborhood, their community. That was how these savage ravaged victims felt.

Driscoll did not derive anything but that there were more of them than him and he didn't care for the odds.

Gesturing at the swarm of babes and influx of mammals, Driscoll screamed to the fellow who had slain the alien, "Do something! Shoot them!" His molars chattered. He felt outnumbered. Like most bullies, he was a coward.

"They're kids. And animals," the man responded. "I have my limits."

"Are you insane? There are no limits here, can't you see?" hectored Missus Drager. "We're all in a sinking boat and you have the bucket, so start bailing us out or else!"

"Yeah, you have the gun!" Spiro prodded. "What are you waiting for? They're about to tear into us!" He wasn't worried about the furballs. Or that the children resembled avaricious goblins. Just that they were short and there were so many of them.

He was also afraid of crowds.

"Nothing I can do, I don't have enough bullets," the mystery man replied. "And I'm not some comic-book superhero. I'm not even a plain hero. I can't save you. Frankly, I don't think anyone can!"

He seemed unconcerned what might happen to them, as well as to himself. With a dejected mug, the guy waded through the circle of vengeful spirits. And wasn't ripped to shreds.

Crowing with glee, Driscoll dared a step. The children glared up at him, eyes wrathful, closing in. He stumbled away, into their taloned grasps. Yowling, the bully threshed a path arms swinging. Spiro and Missus Drager sprang after him.

The trio kept running and passed the man who didn't care plodding in solitude.

Raucous laughter. A chorus of chutters and rowls, grrrrs and mews. The abused army dissolved, but their pain was real.

11

TONKA'S STORY LEFT US in solemn yet enraptured
moods. Even he was astounded by the life he had led
in his younger years. We were surprised, too, he had
only lost eleven. The man's subsequent decades had
been shrunken, curtailed, shorn of profundity. Virtually
lost as well. Feeling disconnected, incomplete, he wasted
time craving that stolen knowledge; the fond memories
and adventures that he believed were missing — that
he believed defined him. He had lived blearily with one
ambition, to fill that simmering void. But knowing us,
he stated now, he had finally opened his heart. Finally
stopped existing in the past, marking his days by a clock
ticking backwards, and started moving forward through
time.

We changed him forever, he told us, and even
knowing who he was did not change the man he had
become. Though he wore the hat of a magician and
carried the wand of a wizard, he was the friend we
knew and loved. Except for his French accent.

"But what should we call you?" asked Juniper.

It was a question the five of us pondered.

The man in the chapeau grinned and hoisted his
hat. "Allo, I am Armond Arno Benoit, but my friends
call me Tonka," he introduced.

We laughed and hugged, then continued our
journey.

I was ecstatic that the five of us were safe and
sound, wending our way through the most spectacular
fable.

On my mind, however, was the nagging fear that this fantasy dimension and its pitfalls was preventing me from fulfilling my father's request. I was being distracted, I felt. But if not for these compelling circumstances, a dear friend would not have been able to achieve his heart's desire. He would not have found his story.

My own heart was encumbered by a wish that could not be granted. Instead of my past, I had lost my parents. How could they ever be replaced?

Rhonda squeezed my hand. "Why are you so sad?"

I was smiling outwardly. Somehow she had sensed it, although I was supposed to be the intuitive one.

"I don't know," I fibbed, not wanting to ruin the moment. "Why do you only wear red?"

"You got me!" the girl shrugged.

"There must be an explanation," I probed.

"Nope, there isn't. Maybe I just like it. Not everyone has a mystery to solve!"

"Are you sure? I have the stone. You have red," I listed. "We don't know why Rupert is a dog or Juniper a tree."

"Arf," confirmed Rupert.

"You're right, we don't." Rhonda gave a nod, lips compressed.

"Perhaps you like red because it connects to somezing," suggested Tonka.

"Like tomatoes," Juniper supplied. "You love pizza."

"Mmm, I do! But I don't think that's it."

"There must be something," I prompted. "A repressed memory. An incident or object you forgot . . ."

Halting, Rhonda scrunched her eyes shut. We paused with her. Then peered expectantly when her eyelids flapped up.

"Well?" I interrogated.

"I guess it could be linked to my chain gum-chewing.
Which I'm not doing because I'm out of gum, and which
I began to end my compulsive nail-biting. It worked!
But I still pick them," she confessed. She was doing it
then, digging at a fingernail of one hand with a fingernail
on the other, chipping off strips to trim the nubs.
"I started the nail habit to rid myself of a nervous
eye-twitch."

"But why? What made you so jittery?" I ferreted.

"Well, the eye thing started because of the bull."
Ronnie sketched arcs with her forefingers as she talked.

My nose tingled. That meant trouble. "What bull?"

"The cantankeroustic fiercest bull ever!" Rhonda
depicted.

"Oh, that one," I joked.

The girl told us she lived next to a farm. A fenced
pasture bordered the yard where she would swing on
a tire attached by rope to a tree branch. El Matador was
a large black hunk of muscular intensity that occupied
the field. He didn't like her. He didn't like anyone or
anything.

Each day Matador watched her gliding back
and forth or spinning. His eyes were red. His nostrils
snorted above a steel ring. His dark enormity quivered
as he paced the other side of the fence. He'd ram the
planks and posts from an angle, then revert to strutting
again.

On a blustery evening, Ronnie was out there
swinging. She didn't have any playmates nearby and
spent a lot of the time amusing herself. Dusk had set,
the air was brisk, and Matador seemed antsy.

A pickup drove toward the bull and parked,
headlamps spotlighting the unruly beast. A couple
of teenage boys climbed from the cab, slammed their
doors.

El Matador faced them, pawing chunks of turf. The boys had a lariat. They lassoed the bull and tied him to a fencepost. They also had a whip, and a bottle of liquor.

Tipping the bottle to their mouths, laughing, the boys proceeded to beat the bull and taunt him, staying out of his range.

Dry grass and dirt eddied. The riled bull clobbered the fence with his hooves, then bashed it with his horns.

Ronnie sat hanging on, allowing the tire to gravitate to a standstill. She was afraid she might get in trouble for being there, that the boys would come after her.

She could see blood glistening on the persecuted creature's shoulders and haunches in the light. He was more rankled than usual, vellicating, lurching against his tether. She was afraid of him, yet sympathetic. It was brutal, unfair. She hated the boys for what they were doing. She hated bullfights too because, along with the pageantry, bulls were stabbed to death.

Leaving the animal tied, the drunk rowdies swaggered to their truck and fumbled within. One cranked the ignition. The engine flooded.

The afflicted bull wrenched free, dragging part of the fence down. He barreled at the truck, caving the grill. A headlamp shattered. His ensuing charge, the second light splintered. The ruffians were screaming. The pickup reversed chased by the bull. The vehicle attempted to turn, braking to shift. The passenger door was gored. The truck rolled. The bull smashed the cab until it was demolished.

His fury untamed, the embittered beast trotted to the hole in the fence. His leash had shed its appurtenances. He sighted Rhonda clinging to the tire and scuffed clods of soil, prepping for a final mad dash.

She was paralyzed by terror. As the galled mass of locomotion bore down, Rhonda's father snatched her from the swing and retreated inside.

He then gripped a shotgun, in case the beast imposed his ire on the house.

The bull receded across the fence-line, where he mellowly grazed in his pasture. Rhonda never saw him again.

"Do you think he could be why I wear red?" she questioned. "Because I'm scared of bulls?"

"But then you *shouldn't* wear that color," I corrected. "According to tradition, bulls are *provoked* by seeing red."

"Oh, I had it backwards!" Ronnie exclaimed. "I've been doing it all wrong!"

"Zat's just a myth," Tonka elucidated. "Bull hooey!"

Rhonda inferred: "I'd always swing in a bright red coat. And Matador didn't go berserk until the day I had to wear a blue jacket so my red one could be washed. I guess that's why I thought the red protected me."

"Well, now you can wear any color you want," I avouched.

"But red is still my favorite!" she predicated.

Four of us laughed. Rupert barked.

"Another riddle answered." I touched Junebug's arm. "Why are you named for a tree?"

Juniper's twinkling eyes grew serious. "Dat is not a pleasant story."

"Oh, like mine was fun?" reproved Ronnie.

"I didn't say it was!" Junebug groaned. "All right, if you must know, but it isn't a mystery. My moder named her daughters after trees to keep dem safe. She believed de spirit of each tree was a guardian, sworn to protect one person or family. As we cut down da forests, we are losing our protectors."

"So that's it? That's your story? It's nice, but I think you have more to tell," I coaxed. "Let's hear the unpleasant part."

Sighing, Juniper related that when her mother was pregnant with her first child, soldiers invaded the village. Kamaria and her husband Badru escaped, hiding inside an old fat baobab's trunk situated amidst a forested belt of corkwood, mangrove, apa, kola nut, and other trees.

Wails and gunfire. The soldiers kidnapped women and children, then drove away in military transports. Men who resisted the raid had been murdered.

The couple crept out. Their village was in hysterics. It was a nightmare they could never forget.

Six daughters were born: Baobab, Mikoko, Sapele, Kola, Mpira, and Mreteni. Soldiers came back. Mreteni's mother and she hid in the hollow tree and were spared. Juniper's sisters, playing with friends at the far edge of the village, were abducted. She wouldn't see them again. Her father was killed defending the children.

Juniper was scarcely a teenager when more trucks rolled into her community. She and her mother absconded to their sanctuary. One of the uniformed thugs bearing automatic weapons spied them running and followed. They could hear his footsteps crunch toward their refuge and embraced each other tightly. The askari smoked a cigarette, leaning against the tree, as he listened for movement. Acrid odor penetrated a rift in the bark and burned Juniper's nostrils. Before she could suppress it with her palms, she sneezed.

The man with the rifle flushed them out, marched them to a canopy-covered truck. The ride was bumpy, chilling. Gusts swirled the sand in their wake, rising, accumulating. Molding features, to Mreteni's youthful imagination. The mystical face winked.

They arrived at a camp and were sequestered: Juniper with the girls, her mother with the older women assigned to chores. Boys would be taught to shoot, and to hate their own families.

Hope of reuniting with their five sisters and daughters instantly fizzled. The girls must have gone to a separate site. Or worse. Awful things were done to the females for the amusement of the soldiers; they were tortured and abused while the men smoked and drank and laughed. Scarred internally and externally, Mreteni survived; her mother did not.

"My family, my childhood were taken away," the woman lamented. "Mama was wrong. A tree would not protect us. It could only be dere."

"Sometimes that's enough," I softly stated. "And sometimes we need more."

I hugged my friend, who shook decades after. The experiences were emblazoned on her psyche forever. She couldn't erase the horror. But she could let go of the pain. And the terror.

"It wasn't your fault," I instinctively apprised.

Juniper thanked me, eyes wet with unshed tears. "I see dat now. I couldn't den. I have not spoken of dis. It was very heavy. I feel a burden has been lifted." She nodded. "I have an alphabet soup of conditions — ways dat keeping dis inside has affected me! I will be better. Perhaps not whole. But I will be all right. I will no longer be afraid."

We traded smiles. Rhonda, Terence, and Tonka clasped Junebug one by one. Sniffing, brushing a tear from her cheek, she admonished us to quit fussing over her.

I reflected to myself how Tonka had spent his life trying to remember his past, while Juniper had spent hers trying to forget. They had both lost a lot of being in the present.

Rupert's tale remained. We all knew mine. We were living it.

Terence flashed a shy grin. I had a feeling that his story would be the strangest. Indeed it was.

"My parents were absent-minded geniuses," he revealed. "We visited a museum when I was three. I was entranced by an exhibit of dinosaurs. I thought the skeletons were jigsaw puzzles, and I started piecing them apart then putting them together. Nobody seemed to notice, least of all Mom and Dad, who were engrossed in a debate about the accuracy of a hominid display. Some of the bones were difficult to unwire. I didn't see that the pair had wandered off upon settling their discussion. It completely fled their minds that they had brought me with them, and took them days to even realize they had a son, once I was no longer there as a reminder!"

By the time he assembled the T-Rex, brontosaurus and stegosaurus (rectifying them a bit), everyone had departed — including Marv and Myrna Hacklehoff, his parents, who were by then immersed in another dialogue. So Terence tottered around by himself for seventy-two hours rearranging artifacts, playacting with relics, swiping the lunches of guards and docents.

Bored, the precocious nipper borrowed a phone on the Information Desk to call home. He left a message for his parents to pick him up at their earliest convenience.

It was thirty-two hours before Myrna and Marv blew in. They had been busy with work and dusting their collection of Pre-Columbian pots. The couple asked for Terence in the lobby. None of the staff had seen him. Marv recalled that their instructions were to claim their son at the baggage room. They procured him and that was that.

Until . . . a few months later, the family took a day off for a trip to the zoo. An altercation arose between the Doctors Hacklehoff over whether the Pronghorn Antelope should be classified an antelope, a goat, an antelope-goat, or deserved to be in a unique category. The couple again neglected their son, ambling to the successive habitat without him.

They argued the same topic the entire afternoon, then exited the gate and immediately changed the subject. Terence, meanwhile, had busied himself with reporting violations of the no-feeding-animals policy: yanking the pant-legs or knee-socks of keepers, who were too distrait themselves to wonder why a dinky three-year-old was unaccompanied.

Aware he had been re-abandoned, the moppet determined to make the best of his stay and see some of the animals up-close and personal. He swung from ropes with monkeys and chimps, made faces with an orangutan, rode bear-back, and napped in a vacant kangaroo pouch like a joey.

Terence played tug-of-war with an elephant's trunk, sunbathed atop a tortoise, tumbled with hyenas, and slid on his belly with the penguins. He was busted when a zoo patron asked a staff member if the little boy sleeping with the gorillas was a mutated ape. The tyke was chastened to phone home.

His biologicals showed up within forty-eight hours. It was a bad time for them, being cranberry season. They were examining the effects of gamma rays on reddish fruit. (Not for any scientific purpose; strictly for something to do.)

The third time they forgot him was at the library. Terence was reading a suspenseful book on how to build your own life-support system, when he looked up to find that his parents had checked out their voluminous stacks of tomes and meandered off without him.

That was the final insult. Deeming them unfit, he ran away. From the library and, indirectly, from home.

A flea-bitten mongrel named Gwendolyn befriended the urchin and led him to a warehouse in which resided other outcasts. Terence consented to be raised by this pack of stray dogs. He was respected by the curs as if he were a mutt himself. To fit in, he copied their behavior. They dubbed him Rupert.

For seven years he lived as a canine. It was there he found acceptance; he felt happy and safe. That feeling never leaves you, like a warm security blanket, or hugging a teddy-bear. But then he was discovered, a feral vagrant dog-boy. Local media hyped his picture in the news.

The Doctors Hacklehoff recognized him because he was a ten-year-old version of his father, except for the eye patch, with his bushy curls and sparrow beak. (It was really a nose.)

They took him to their lab to study, like some alien or unidentified species. Terence didn't care for sleeping in a cage. He broke out and combed the streets, wanting to rejoin his pack. They had been evicted from the warehouse. The lad feared they were captured like him, hauled to a pound. He searched the streets and animal shelters to no avail.

His biological family tracked him down. They inveigled that his fur family was in their lab, being used for research. Terence was coerced to return with the scientists, his former parents. He hoped to retrieve the dogs.

He was strapped to a table. His friends were in pens but swatches of hair were shaved, their bodies and heads connected to wires. Some of the canines had been surgically mutilated. Their puppy-dog eyes beseeched Rupert to help them. Cats, primates, and other guinea pigs were obscenely scourged. The boy was laden with despair.

Then an animal-rights group stormed in, rescuing Rupert and all of the victims, who would be nursed back to health. His biologicals were incarcerated, charged with child neglect and abuse. (It wasn't against the law to use animals for testing, as long as they were "properly" fed and maintained.)

The strays were adopted by loving human families. Terence was sent to a foster home. He was too much like a dog, the substitute parents complained.

He'd be shuttled to another home, where people said they wanted to *cure* him.

After deplorable experiences with humans, the boy just wanted to be a dog. The pack had been the only place that he felt he belonged.

Conscious he had new friends, however, Terence didn't need to be a hound anymore. "I might take a crack at being human. They're not all of them so dreadful," he had to admit.

My nose still tingled. Something bad was imminent. "Come on," I said, "let's keep going before —"

My sentence was interrupted by the bad thing. Or things, rather, being several of them.

You know how your days can be uneventful, utterly bland and banal, and then everything seems to happen at once? We suddenly perceived a horrid clattering and found ourselves cringing in a crossroads that hadn't been there a minute ago.

On the left stampeded a rhinoceros, only this fella boasted the lateral horns of a bull as well as a set of snout tusks.

To the right rolled a shiny black robotic army of one, laser turret blasting on his dome, machine-gun rounds sputtering from his arms, motorized treads propelling him toward us.

Ahead rushed three of my neighbors. How they got in front of us I'll never know.

And behind came a dude with metal-rim glasses in a stained lab coat, rubber gloves up to his elbows, fleeing his own creation: the stitched-together staggering Monster he had depravedly engineered from corpses. These retro classic grayscale icons appeared to be transferred out of a late-night movie.

I have no clue what we'd've done if Tonka didn't aim his magic wand and beam us up. There wasn't even time to pray.

12

ANZILLU'S APPETITE FOR VAGARY was unsated, his odium unabated. There was a proverb among these cliff-dwelling primitive plebes with their fabricated mountain structures, their tedious feuds and squabbles and scrabblings for greatness, that an ill wind blows no good. Who were they to speak of the wind? They knew nothing with their tiny brains and temporal lives! How could they dare pretend to be any more than a gnat to a spirit of his lofty status? Despicable pests! They were nothing but a botched and worthless science experiment; a disease that had been permitted to flourish and infect a once-healthy thriving planet. His planet.

He was weary of having to overlook their excess, forgive their trespasses, because they were supposed to be intelligent and compassionate! Where were these sublime qualities when they were so busy destroying the garden and sky and sea that they were bestowed? The swines comported like spoiled brats!!! the tempest raged. They were self-centered, foolish and corrupt. Besides that, they were vulgar and petty and frustrating!

And yet there were those who felt they had merit. A rain spirit (not *the* Rain, a lesser) had obsequiously contended: "They're not so bad once you get to know them. It's so cute how they waddle about in snowsuits and mittens. I used to love their yellow coats, the rubber boots and galoshes! Their umbrellas are adorable! You really shouldn't turn those inside-out, you know. That isn't very nice."

"Bah!" jeered Anzillu.

"Not all appreciate rainy days, but others sing in the rain or dance for it," lauded the sprinkler. "There are bad ones, yes. But many are good. Some are merely nescient, unenlightened. You should give them a chance!"

A chance? When they had reduced the vibrant gem of the universe, a lush paradise of wonders and bounty, into a congested ailing organism that would surely perish without drastic intervention? He had cautioned them with tornadoes and hurricanes and other hints, only to be ignored. Why should he bother? He ought to let them nullify themselves at their own hands!

The demon wind had in mind to wage a one-jinn war if the blighters didn't clean up their act. But his motives were not unselfish. He had more narcissistic goals at his crux. There was a cosmic order to the universe, and a hierarchy to everything. Planets had tiers of power, from the physical to the spiritual, regulating who ate who and what each force could or couldn't do. These pyramids of administration and jurisdiction were complex. Even ants had their own chain of command.

Ara-Alal-Alad-Ab-Zu-Apsu was an ambitious spirit. Bound to Earth, he hoped that harnessing the stone would gain him advantage in challenging The Prime Elements: Wind, Rain, Earth, and Fire. He was already mightier than The North Wind.

Power struggles were constant. Just as Evil, ruler of The Underworld, was eternally striving to defeat Good, The Sovereign Spirit, and designate all Fates. Anzillu wished to magnify his abilities with those of The Elements, as his powers had been augmented by the stone. At the same time that it was his weakness, the rock would be his greatest asset.

The stone had made him a singular unnatural force with no perch in the pecking order. He had to bully his way into the line-up — establish his own roost. And it wasn't going to be at the bottom!

Perhaps he was curious. Perhaps simply bored.
It was his further intention to evaluate whether these
lowly fleshbags deserved another chance. Or if he
should huff and puff them off the face of the earth.
The jaundiced zephyr believed the planet would be
well rid of their miserable lot.

His ever-evolving and revolving playground
would have to be revved up a notch, he gloated,
the gait accelerated. No more pussyfooting around.
It was time for some higher sport. Let the games
begin.

BOOK TWO

THE EYE OF THE STORM

13

THE ZOMBIE OWL who stole my beret coasted by
overhead, preening, ragged wings outspread. It was
my best beret so I ran like the wind, deaf to protests.
Curving through tunnels, I swiftly found myself
disoriented. I had been divided from my companions,
with no idea how to locate them, just after we were
elevated to another story of the labyrinth.

My beret was dropped as a consolation prize.
I felt duped. "Thanks a lot." Dourly I scooped up my
cap.

The owl sailed off, hooting at my expense.

"Stupid bird," I complained. Perhaps I should have
felt sorry for the thing. It *was* dead. But I wasn't in the
mood to be empathetic.

Listening, I tried to ascertain if I could hear the
voices of my friends. The walls were vapor-thin, after all.

No dice. There was a subliminal howl like a chinook
whipping through my ears; like standing at the summit
of an extremely tall mountain. I tried to call out so they
might hear. My voice was whisked away by a breeze.

"Oh come on!" I shouted, steaming. This place
was really starting to irk me! "What do you want?
Why am I here? Why are you doing this to us?"

Everything got quiet. Even the howl.

"Explain yourself or release me!" I yelled. "I will
not serve as a patsy for your convoluted kicks!"

Lo and behold, the storm effect modified and
I stood in the middle of an ordinary road lined by
majestic evergreens. The sun had gone down.

A signpost held a white shield bearing a big black zero.

I scowled in disbelief at the placard. This made no more sense than the other place, the windworld. It might look normal. But it was not the hallway of my building. Or anywhere close. And, I skepted, Highway Zero didn't sound very promising!

Shambling forth, I adjusted the strap of my dark-blue messenger bag. I had forgotten I brought it, the canvas sack was so unobtrusive.

My fleece jacket failed to prevent a shiver. Icy wind buffeted, and my dark hair lashed a cheek. I tucked the locks behind an ear and snugged my beret down. It was going to be a cold walk, and I didn't know where I was going, whether I should head in this direction or turn around.

The reason I left my room in the first place seemed to be the last thing on my mind since stepping out the door. This day was more mixed up than most. And yet — tears stung my eyes — I had discovered amazing things about my friends! I may have gotten them and myself lost; I might be way off-course, but for a while it didn't matter.

A chill passed through me. I felt alone.

That indomitable spirit of adventure I had inflated like a balloon sprung a leak. Self-pity sluiced my veins. Where was I going? I was roaming a strange countryside, and I didn't know how to get back to my friends!

Twin torches stabbed out of the night as an air-horn blared. A logging truck roared at me. I jumped in fright then scrambled aside, cutting my knees on gravel. Straightening, I flicked pebbles from torn jeans and skin. The truck rumbled away, careening wildly with a cargo of timber.

"Crazy driver!" I muttered. What else did I need?

Apparently, gobs of rain.

My clothes quickly grew saturated, as if a lake or river in the heavens were overflowing on my head. Shoes squeaking, denim chafing along the road, I was informed by a sign it was thirteen miles to Woebegone.

Thirteen miles? I would never make it tonight. And I wasn't sure that I wanted to, even if I could, judging by the town's name!

Halting, I considered ducking below a tree. But it might rain for hours. I needed to find a phone and call my aunt, to verify that it wasn't her I saw being sucked into the cyclone. I needed to call the cops to help the people who were! Maybe there would be a house. A roadside tavern or diner. A gas station. I was an optimist so I kept squishing forward. And arrived at the gate to a cemetery.

Not quite what I was hoping for. Still, perhaps there was a mausoleum or caretaker's office. I entered the graveyard. I know, dumb move. *Really* dumb, as it turned out.

Heed my advice: Don't ever stroll between columns of tombstones on a dark and stormy night. Stay home. Lock your doors and windows. Draw the curtains.

Stepping on a mushy path, I was a bundle of nerves. My eyes darted side to side as I tremblingly trod toward a stone structure. All the usual fears crowded my cranium: the walking dead, the undead, the dead dead. I didn't want to meet any of them!

Rain ceased.

I could then divine the scrape and shuff-thud of digging. It meant that somebody in this godforsaken place was alive! Nearing the rhythmic activity, I observed a man in black stooped to the task.

"Hi there!" I greeted. A bit too jolly for the occasion. The guy jolted as if he'd been caught at something illicit. I didn't care *what* he was up to — digging a grave, exhuming a body, interring someone . . . I just wanted to use a phone!

The Gravedigger

I was one of the few individuals in the world who didn't carry the device with me at all times. Believe it or not, since the accident, I didn't like talking on telephones.

Back to the gravedigger. Or grave robber, whatever the case might be. The portly man, vested in a funereal cape over his drab suit, was not elated to see me. Tossing his shovel, he flailed from the pit and scurried off shrieking. I guess he wasn't expecting company.

In retrospect, I can't blame him. The living do not generally frequent cemeteries at night. Then, however, I was highly offended. I was also sodden, exhausted, and almost as cold as a cadaver. "Hey!" I squawked. "You don't have to be rude!"

I approached the entrance of the building, fingers crossed for a pay-phone or reception desk inside. These things never go well. You can't just waltz into a crypt without a hammer and some stakes, cloves of garlic, and an axe or chainsaw! That's just basic in these situations. I was inexperienced at surviving horror scenes, what can I say?

The door, of course, creaked. My steps echoed on a marble floor. "Hello? Is anyone here?" I inquired. No response. That was a good thing. The mausoleum seemed empty except for wall plaques and doors to the coffin chambers. My soles tapped as I strode a distance within. There could be a phone around the corner, I rationalized.

Yeah, right. The mind tempts us with what-ifs when we are at our most desperate and cannot refuse. Don't listen!

There was something past the corner, though it wasn't a phone and I had no wish to touch it. I'm not sure what it was. The creature was brown and bulky. Its body resembled a combination of soil and roots, bones and tendons, coated with translucent slime.

The face was another matter. Hideous does not begin to describe the face. Its skin writhed with a legion of blood-red worms.

The eyes were holes. Baseless and bereft. Darker than black. Gazing into them, part of you was being siphoned. You had to rip your eyes from its contact.

The nose consisted of three small tentacles, vermilion in color, with stingers on the tips ringed by black feelers. Its mouth had suction lips, spider fangs, and a vivid red tongue with a hollow cusp for latching and drinking.

This mauz monster was feasting on a fresh body, the coffin slid out and uncovered. Tissue was being imbibed through the corpse's unstitched and parted lips. My gut heaved. The ogre stared at me with socket voids but didn't falter in his feeding.

I managed to make like the tide and ebb. The thing allowed me to reach the door and barge outside. Then was on me with a nauseating whoosh of bloodlust and musty odor. I fought to extricate myself from roots and muscles twining about my arms and torso. The tongue unfurled, crimson and dank, insinuating through my lips and teeth. I felt it ply and sift, delving as if for specifics. Not draining me yet — *seeking*. The monster wanted more than my life.

At the time, I was less concerned about his attitude. The thing had its tongue in my mouth and planned to digest me like a spider and slurp me for dinner. All I could do was think how unfair that was, how unlucky I felt, and how ugly my date was. I had become a crybaby invertebrate.

It occurred to me that the gravedigger was the creature. They were the same shape. I connected this piece of useless info just before I was lugged across the cemetery and deposited in the open trench.

**The Rutabogey
Alias The Root Monster**

Reclining, gaping up at the thing — which morphed to the man guise to begin spading soil — I wondered who the grave had been dug for. Not that it would change the fact I was being buried alive, but I had a quizzical mind.

Sometimes there are no good alternatives, and to hope for a miracle is all you can do. I starting wishing. Precipitation started pouring. And the man started melting. Miracle or not, you have to agree that it was pretty darn fortunate.

The gravedigger regressed to the dirt devil. His earthen form was transitioning to mud, rinsing to the ground.

I was like a cat and didn't like to get damp — hated swimming, soaking in a tub, and long walks in the rain. But this water splashing in my eyes and nose, requiring me to spit mouthfuls of liquid as I strained to breathe, was never more welcome.

Alas, my relief would soon end. The creature's roots, bones and sinews, and whatever else composed its frame had stayed intact.

Mud was slung in my face. The palsied phobic inertia evaporated then, and I resolved to put up my dukes. This thing was not going to preserve me for a snack if I could help it (I assumed I was being saved for later). So I sat up, rolled to my dinged knees, then hove to my feet. Well, sort of. They submerged in sludge. I forged to the far wall to scale the mire. Soppy sediment eroded as I clambered out of the ditch.

The cretin stalked after me, literally, with stemmish limbs.

My own legs felt lethargic. I jogged as fast as I could. Each step was a hurdle, a maximum effort. I could hear the thing scratching and rustling behind me.

At some point I stumbled, landing before a burnished marker. Chiseled in granite was the name BELINDA OGDEN.

A pasty hand extruded from sod to grip my wrist.
Hot-cold terror imbued me. *Help!* The silent appeal
clogged my brain.

I was wrested to my feet. Roots and tendons
wrapped around me.

For some reason, my hand slipped beneath
the flap of my bag. I can't say what I thought to find.
I hadn't loaded anything but nose wipes, a paperback
book, a notepad and pen, a foldable comb and hairbrush
combo, and some rubberbands. Hardly the gear to bring
for a treasure hunt. My fingers nonetheless encountered
the exact tool needed for trimming a hedge-like beast:
a pair of pruning shears!

The scissors brandished, thanking my lucky stars,
I snipped and clipped away those pesky fibrous tendrils
restraining me then lunged free of the monster. It made
not a peep, other than shaking itself.

I cast a glance over my shoulder to see if I was
being chased and ogled a girl with dark splotches
encircling her eyes, frizzy tresses bedraggled, a white
running suit smudged and torn, her feet bare.

She stood next to the creature, by the headstone
of Belinda Ogden. I blinked and she was gone.

Chugging to the road, I didn't slow down for about
a mile.

14

UNBEKNOWNST TO HER NIECE, Aunt Camille did
indeed enter the storm. She was swept to another vault.
Her close personal friend Doctor Nigel Hurst bruised
her when he landed. "Get off me, you oaf," grunted
Camille, shoving him.

"Sorry, my dear." Nigel gingerly boosted himself
aside. "Where do you think we are?" He adjusted his
spectacles, then his bolo tie (a gift from Camille, who
wanted him to look more snazzy).

"I don't know, and I'm sure I don't care." Camille
primped her cropped and permed hairdo. "But I am
thinking to sue someone, for wrinkling my outfit!"
She was wearing an expensive dress-suit. "Plus,
my designer purse is nowhere in sight!"

"Not to worry, you always look stunning," Nigel
flattered.

"Yes, I know. But sometimes it isn't easy," griped
Camille. "There's the wind, and the rain, and the sun.
There's dust and pollen, humidity. I really hate the
elements!"

"Well, you can't sue *them*," quipped Nigel.

"Too bad," Camille croaked. The doctor assisted
her to stand. Smoothing her skirt, she hiked the lapels
of her jacket and drew a cleansing breath. "Well, let's
get back to what we were doing, shall we?"

"Certainly." Nigel escorted her from the chamber
onto a path.

The couple moseyed for a spell. "Everything's the same. Are we actually getting somewhere?" Camille was not very patient.

Nigel, her beau, wished she would stop nattering. He was preoccupied with dreams of wealth. In particular, he had always wanted a gold tooth like a pirate. Since losing a few of his front teeth, being walloped in the mouth by a mental case, he decided that he ought to have three! It would be quite debonair, he imagined.

"Are you listening to me?"

"Of course! What was that again?" The gold teeth would go swell with his goatee, Doctor Hurst hankered.

"Honestly! You're completely ignoring me!" cavilled Camille.

"Not completely." *Oops.* Giving a wan grin, the doctor was about to ask again what it was he had missed when he discerned there was no trail underfoot. They seemed to be walking on air!

But that was impossible. Hurriedly, Nigel leaped to where the passage had abruptly been cut off, then graciously stretched an arm toward his lady-friend. "My dear, you mustn't panic," he stated in his deep hypnotic voice. "Take hold of my hand and everything will be fine."

Camille demanded to know why she shouldn't panic. And why he was over there, when he had been beside her a moment ago!

She then perspected the absence of a path. "What the dickens?" And gawped straight down. That was the wrong thing to do. Her mind reeled with a burst of dizziness and she dropped.

Nigel, poised on the verge, rubbed a whiskered chin. "Hmmm." The doc elected to go after her or he would never hear the end of it. He took a step. And didn't fall.

Camille was plummeting pronto. She should've lunched on fruit instead of a baked potato, she chided. Even though she was exceptionally thin and it wouldn't have made much difference. She was a stickler for details, and in these situations an ounce of prevention was worth a pound of potato. Or something like that.

Nigel hopped. He stamped his shoe. The air held firm. This was most peculiar. He couldn't seem to find a soft spot.

Camille, despite the velocity of her descent, had plenty of time to contemplate the history of monks in Tibet; the migrations of Monarch Butterflies; and the annoying detour this was sure to impose — unless she wound up on the outside of the inside of wherever they were after being vacuumed into that confounded draft. It was all such an inconvenience!

Nigel shuffled back to the passage, made some practice runs, then took a flying leap off the edge. He hugged his knees in midair, eyes shut tight. And dangled above where the path used to extend. Eyelids raised, he craned to peek below in surprise.

Camille wasn't accustomed to nonsense. Her life was implicitly organized. She had scant tolerance for silliness or abstraction or *dis*-traction.

She was a plain-and-simple person, although she was neither plain-featured nor simple-minded. She just didn't like weirdities. She didn't even like the *word* "weirdity" because it wasn't an official term.

The doctor unhugged his legs then uncrimped them. He waved his extremities as if to imprint a snow angel where there wasn't any snow. Or any anything! *This is rather odd,* he ruminated. And leaned forward.

To his alarm, he flipped so his feet were up and his head faced down. Endeavoring to swim, Nigel's suspension suspended and he was nosediving to a misty nadir.

He bellowed, limbs fanning. The befuddled shrink positively shrank in fear as the base of his topple arrived.

Camille's decline halted too. In an instant she was placed on a gameboard with squares delineated along a trail. She tried to stray from the path but couldn't. She also couldn't move to another tile. She had to wait her turn.

"I hate games!" she cried, clenched fists upthrust to the sides. The board tremored. She skimmed forth seven spaces.

The instructions at her feet augured: *Walk on your hands and count to three, or you'll wish you had.*

"Why would I wish that?" Camille mumbled, squinting at the letters. "Don't tell me what to wish!"

A card from a regular-sized deck, disproportionate to the gameboard, was slapped on her brow. She peeled it off and read, "Don't say I didn't warn you." Camille tutted, "What kind of absurd drivel is this?" And discarded the card. "As if I'm attired for walking on my hands!" she grumbled.

The woman was bopped and plopped to disparate sectors of the board like a checker, then schussed over numerous squares and plastered to a door that blocked her path. Camille couldn't help noticing scarlet letters painted on black: SAY KNOCK KNOCK.

Spurning the obvious directions, she attempted to turn the knob. Bedlam. Gongs. Lights and sirens.

A hand to her mouth, she hastily rapped her knuckles on wood. The door failed to open. The tumult continued.

Flustered, the woman hammered a fist and jerked the knob. "Let me in!"

Nigel sauntered up behind her, massaging his nose as if he'd landed on it. "What's this?" He stepped around the barrier.

"Hah!" Camille was miffed that she didn't think of that. But then the portal flew to expulse the interloper into her arms. "Hah!" she repeated, with an I-told-you-so emphasis. Even though she hadn't.

The door slammed. Nigel tugged at the knob.

Reading the advisory, the doctor gargled and uh-hummed. "Knock, knock!" he conceded.

Camille didn't think of that either. Oh well, he *was* more educated. She only had a degree in knitting. The scrap of paper hadn't helped to advance her career as a toe masseuse. No wonder she had so few clients. Everything was about credentials and certificates these days!

Meanwhile the door swung wide, reacting to the magic words.

"Hmmph! I was about to try *Open Sesame*. I bet that would've worked just as well," sniffed Camille.

"This isn't a competition, my dear. Although it is a game so it might be," mollified her boyfriend. He was actually her fiancé, but that was hush-hush. Camille didn't want her niece to know about him yet because he was treating the girl for Anxiety and Fatigue. It was one of many secrets Camille had been keeping from Arletta. She felt the poor thing couldn't handle too much excitement.

"*Life* is a competition, Nigel. And I play to win!" Camille hooked his elbow and towed him over the threshold. She had forgotten about the glum prognostication should she balk at walking on her hands. It was ridiculous anyway!

She wanted to proceed with these frivolous rules so they could quit being sidetracked and get back to their plans! But rules are rules and she had learned that it was wiser to obey some of the rules some of the time, which left the rest of the time to be naughty. And scheme at not getting caught!

The couple promenaded as if they owned the game. Rich as they yearned to become, perhaps they would. A life-sized gameboard was a catchy theme. But a square marked PREPARE TO MEET YOUR DOOM was stickier than a wicketous clump of molasses. They couldn't pass. They couldn't pick up their feet.

"Now what?" Camille and Nigel were equally flummoxed.

A female hippopotamus clad in a sweatshirt abeled FELICITY wembled along on her hind-legs as if it were perfectly common for a hippo to wear clothes. "Hello," she trebled and kept going.

"Excuse us, but what are we supposed to do?" Camille implored.

The plump soprano warbled as she wiffled away from them that it wasn't any of her business what they were doing or should do or had done when she didn't even know who they were.

"Oh!" Camille was nigh speechless as the critter flumphed off.

Nigel patted the top of her hand in a conciliatory manner. "There, there," he soothed.

Camille freed her hand, cheeks florid. "What a lot of nerve!" she spumed. "And don't tell me *there* when it's your fault that I'm being snubbed by *animals*!"

Nigel rolled his eyes. "Yes, dear." He then had a brilliant idea that involved removing their shoes.

The pair sashayed onward in stockings, their footwear abdicated. Camille stepped on a space that was a trapdoor and rapidly disappeared. Nigel, who was not very attentive, planted a sock on the same square before realizing she was gone.

In this game, the penalty for noncompliance was a plunge to the dungeon. Nigel had "dumbled" onto the pratfall, triggering this humiliating episode, by accident. Not that he was a dumbbell. At times he merely wasn't very smart.

Being in the dungeon had its advantages. Things couldn't get much worse, for one thing. Well, that was probably the only thing.

Camille smacked the bald spot at the highest point on his head, not that his head was pointed — which was probably bald from her whacking it.

"What are you doing?" the shrew ranted. "You were supposed to stay up there! How are you going to rescue me from down here?"

"Now that you mention it, I hadn't thought about that," remarked Nigel.

"You never think!" railed Camille. "I have to do all of the thinking for you and me both!"

Nigel thought to himself that it wasn't that he didn't think, it was that he often thought about the wrong thing.

"And you never listen!" accused Camille when she noticed that his eyes were glazed from thinking rather than hearing her subsequent grievance that he didn't listen, which he consequently didn't hear, proving her point.

It was prudent, he found sometimes, to ignore her so that she would be right and he would be happy — ignorance being bliss.

Camille jacked her jaw to reprehend him for an infraction that he hadn't even done yet, but she presumed he was bound to commit sooner or later, when a low-set metallic door scrooched up at the bottom of a wall and a spinner was pushed in. The grate banged down.

The prisoners regarded the game prop with suspicion. It sat there before them, intriguing and inscrutable. No symbols or letters distinguished it, other than numerals for the spinner to indicate.

"Go on," Nigel invited. "Ladies first."

"Men only say that when they're too cowardly to go themselves," was Camille's deft parry.

"Ouch." The smirksome doctor flicked the plastic arrow with an index finger. "Seven. Your turn, my dear."

Camille gave the spinner a half-hearted nudge. The tip landed on a line between digits. She gave it another twirl. Thirteen. Larger than seven.

The woman beamed victorious. The panel rose in a jiffy. A small robotic bird hummed in. The gadget herkily buzzed to Camille and emoted, "Your number is up!"

Getting tired of receiving these dire predictions, she batted the bird out of her way and crawled to the door from whence it propelled. She was tall yet built like a reed and fancied that she could fit through the opening, which was still open. Some of her could and some of her couldn't. She became wedged.

Nigel was left with the better half, her backside. The end that could harp and carp was somewhere else, being condemned by a jury of her peers at which she was peering — in three looking-glasses that contained her face.

"You should talk!" she garrulously told herself. "You're no better than I am!"

The mice who were holding the mirrors up so she could come to this conclusion blindly carried the looking-glasses away.

An ostrich perambled to her and cleared his throat. This took awhile since his throat was lengthy. At last he bade without so much as a preamble, "Off with your head."

Camille stared flakily about for a guillotine; a hooded man with an axe. "It doesn't come off," she pled. And wrangled to extract herself from the hole.

"Never a naysayer be!" scalded the ostrich. "If you're not going to cooperate, you'll have to be banished."

"Banished? From here? I think I'd like that," Camille assayed. "But it's going to be a little difficult since I seem to have gotten myself stuck!"

"Ditchdiggers!" heralded the ostrich.

Too late. Meerkats were already excavating with picks and spades below Camille's waist. Once she felt the tautness relax, the woman called to her fiancé to pull her ankles.

Nigel had been napping, snoring cartoonishly, using her rump as a pillow. Yawning, he obliged and she popped free. They were remanded to Start, which was where the board finished. The game was over and they had lost.

15

MY BONEYARD FLIGHT led me to a dirt lane branching off the highway. I was skittish about venturing from the beaten path, having just been molested by something with twigs for brains. Whatever had been in the graveyard, I was not very anxious to meet its cousin.

And then again, it was twelve miles to the next town. It might behoove me to check this out, I conjectured. So there I went. As if I, too, had twigs for smarts.

The road wound into the trees. I couldn't see what lay before me, but mercifully the squall had terminated. You can only get so wet. After that, you begin to pucker.

Slopping along the muddy trail, steering around puddles, I passed what appeared to be an abandoned jalopy. The old gas-guzzler was parked parallel to the lane. I couldn't survey its interior; glass was covered with muck and moisture. The rear plate had a vanity tag: OKTOGON. I thought about claiming the rectangle as a souvenir of this rambunctious night. Was the misspelled word an indirect reference to Stop Signs? It seemed kind of strange so I left the plate alone.

Air was frigid and wild, flirting with my hair, knifing through humid fabric. I felt like an ice queen, my soul to the depths of me frozen solid.

My nose started to bleed. It happens as a premonition, when there's something turbulent in store. I had a nosebleed the day my parents took a drive off a cliff.

That should have been sufficient to dissuade my course. You'd think. I was really not in my right mind, I guess, because I kept going. Riffling through my bag, I confiscated a wad of tissue paper and blotted it to my nasal cavities. It wasn't a runny nose, I determined.

Twenty or so steps past the clunker, I heard creaking like the hinges of a car door. The disturbance sent a glacial stream of terror up my spine! I quit moving, then turned slowly. Mistake Number Two. I should've run. Mistake Number One, of course, was walking down that unpaved road.

None of the doors had budged. Sighing, I wheeled to resume splodging. The retinal image of a man-sized silhouette caused a screech within. Drawing a breath, puffing heavily, I swung toward the rust-heap. Nothing. What the heck? I was in no mood for games — for tiptoeing around and playing peek-a-boo with some shrouded figure!

"Okay, I don't care what I hear or see! I am not going to look!" I stated, faced away from the car.

I risked removing the ball of tissues under my nostrils. No major hemorrhaging. I scanned the vicinity for a trash receptacle. There was only that old car, so I folded the paper to tuck into my bag. It didn't matter if anyone would eyeball me; I was no litterbug.

A warm gush of blood poured over my mouth and chin. "Oh man!" Angling my head forward, I mopped the mess and groped for more tissues, snagging the last of them. As I staunched the flow with paper in my left hand, I pinched my nose above the nostrils with my right thumb and forefinger to put pressure on the vessels.

Bleeding had ceased. That was scary! Stuffing the gory wads inside my canvas pack, I touched a stack of dry tissues. Where did those come from? I culled one to wipe my lips and chin, then creased the paper and applied it to my nostrils. No blood.

That over with, I bowed my bereted head against the wind and trudged on. I didn't get far. That creaking again. I spun to glimpse a man beside the automobile. Yet not one door was open.

This guy was getting on my nerves! I should have been afraid. I was alone and susceptible. He had the advantage of being sinister. But I was indignant after the car shenanigans and my nosebleed.

"Hey!" I called to him. "What's the deal? Are you trying to scare me?"

I certainly was not conducting myself logically. However, nothing about that afternoon or evening had been close to rational. How I ended up in this backwoods bind made absolutely no sense whatsoever! I was supposed to be finding a stone, not some weirdo! My mission had veered well off the nautical charts and here I was, conversing with a strange man — I do mean strange — in a secluded spot by a desolate highway somewhere out in the sticks!

You tell me, was I insane or was this whole thing crazy?

My dander was up, as they say. I verbally accosted the dude without a single thought as to the peril inherent. Yes, I might have been a little bit squirrelly. But crazy is as crazy does! (I think.)

The man, and I use the term loosely, had frizzled gray-black locks to his shoulders and wore a silver robe which dragged in the mud. His features were crude as if sculpted out of clay. Black lips formed an insolent leer. A ratty beard grew to his chest, and a waxen complexion contrasted with the magnitude of his glower.

He drifted towards me, floating slightly off the ground. His arms were protracted, and the hands at his sides were taloned.

Oktogon

By this time, after getting a good look at him (and yes, I swore I wouldn't look but I had to, I just had to), I could see that he was trouble and that I was in trouble and that this was probably the reason for my bloodbath.

Knees clapping together, I couldn't think of any options so I kind of stood there and waited to see what would happen. How could I run from a man who levitates and has clawed fingers? He might not sound too scary but in person, if he was a person, he was pretty creepy!

The guy lifted his arms as if to embrace me. I saw that both palms bore tattoos of eight-sided polygons. My brilliant deductive skills assigned him the identity on the license.

Gleaning his name, if that was his name, emboldened me. "What is it you want?" I demanded (in a mouse-like tone).

An answer issued from Okto's gangrenous lips: "You do not asssk the questionsss!"

I never said it was a good answer. Or the correct one. I was surprised that *he* said anything. Fish teeth like stilettos were visible as he lisped, "What isss yoursss isss mine!"

The bag had been invaluable at the graveyard. I fumbled for those shears. Maybe I could threaten to cut off this guy's beard. But the scissors were ostensibly replaced by the tissues. I had nothing!

A slender tongue lapped over the man's dark lips. He seemed kind of hungry. My feet found traction, my spine the gumption to sprint down the road. I had never been much of a runner, but I gave it my best shot.

To my amazement I was outdistancing him. Or so I thought. He didn't grab me, didn't glissade to intercept my futile strides. Perhaps there was a chance, I dared to believe.

My breaths fogged the cool night air. Hyper steps indiscriminately sloshed over potholes and grime. I didn't care how spattered my jeans or how caked in grunge my shoes, I raced along the road for dear life. And prayed I would find solace around the bend.

That man was no more human than the thing at the cemetery! Had I stumbled into some vast demonic conspiracy? A satanic plot to overthrow the normal world?

Another possibility crowbarred its way into my fevered forehead. Was this part of the curse my father referred to? I hadn't even laid a hand on the stone and it might be turning my life into pandemonium!

Coming to a curve in the road, I wondered if the man lurked beyond my shoulder. I was apprehensive to check, terrified of finding him there. I could detect no sound; not that I expected to hear his footfalls.

There was light, I discovered with a heartened gasp. A faint yellowish gleam. Pounding toward this beacon, this literal ray of hope, I beheld the rough façade of a cabin — the source of the illumination. Increasing my pace, though my side was on fire and my legs felt leaden, I frantically reached the door. Sparing a glance at the road, which was clear up to the bend, I fitfully bruised my knuckles concussing a slab of wood.

"Help!" I called. "Please, I'm lost and there's a man! Please help me! I need to use a phone!"

The door didn't open. The cabin was silent, a single window draped.

"Hello? Is anyone there?" I knocked harder, until my finger joints bled, then attempted to open it myself. The portal appeared to be bolted from within. I could break the window, but the man or whatever he was would get in too.

It was a cruel deception. I sagged against the door. Then percepted movement. A shadow had crossed the lit drape.

"Please let me in!" Another volley of blows.

The door wrenched wide. A pale sweating fortyish blonde with a cautious expression blinked out at me. "Yes?" she asked, barely above a whisper. She seemed frightened.

Given my slovenly condition, I probably looked like a crazy person.

"I'm lost, and there was a man by the road," I explained. "He was —"

"Behind you," she interrupted, eyes dull.

My stomach sank to my toes. I had to turn. How could I not? Had to face my fear. The man was there, shaggy mane and beard glistening from a drizzle that snuck up as quietly as he did. His grin was mordant and triumphant.

Moving with unearthly grace, he forced me backwards into the cabin beside the woman and hovered with his eerie smile, as if admiring his trophies. I gaped at my fellow hostage, who tarried docile and unflinching.

By an oil lamp's golden haze, I witnessed that the woman's neck bore a large wound from a bite of many pointed teeth. Was he some mutant breed of vampire? A knot of tension constricted the base of my gut, along with cold roiling nausea.

The morbid degenerate sprouted four surplus appendages like a spider. He was nearly all arms, a formidable opponent. I did not see how I could escape his clutches — especially when he had twice as many now! His license plate fit very well, I inferred.

The blonde woman didn't need convincing. She was bound to him, surrendering herself mind and body, submitting to his embrace and his kiss, a sacrificial bride. The goon's mouth fastened on the side of her throat as he crushed her to him. He whined, a prolonged squeal of pleasure amidst voracious feasting.

The woman's flesh blanched, losing what vitality hadn't yet been drained. He completed his meal and allowed her corpse to slump.

I was going to be dessert.

The octo-monster's eyes intensified, commanding my will to slacken. I could feel myself melt into obedience, unable to resist. He glided to me and his tentacle-limbs danced with synchronized ripples. It was like a mating rite of birds, the male exhibiting his courtship techniques. I was bizarrely mesmerized, almost catatonic. I felt myself drawn to him, magnetically charged, physically compelled, before his serpentine arms slithered about my torso and I was actually flattened to the creature.

I could sense him probing like rude fingers inside my brain.

Hysterical, my cerebrum rebelled. The stupor dissolved. My hand plumbed defensively into my trusty bag. This time I didn't find wispy tissues. I hauled out the quintessential vampire buzz-killer: a wooden stake. Don't ask me where it came from. I didn't know and didn't care. Tonka had a magic wand. I guessed I had a magic bag.

The octo-man's lips spread, unsheathing rows of vicious fangs. I hefted the stake and drove it in with all of my strength — but not his chest. I shoved it down his gaping maw.

And to think that my aunt believed me incapable of coping under pressure! She seemed to think I was a fragile porcelain doll or vase to be kept on display.

The venal bloodsucker's lips oozed dark liquid. His eyes protruded. The tentacles slid off me. I pushed him and he thudded to the floor of the cabin. Feeling ill, I stepped over the woman and aversely took my leave.

Oktogon was still alive. I heard a gagging moan on my way out the door. With a stake crammed in his gullet, I didn't think he'd be much of a danger.

Oktogon Too

That was close, I marveled. I had survived more trauma in a night than anyone deserved in a lifetime! Plodding brusquely up the muddy road back to the highway, I mused that things could only get better.

As I passed the monster's vehicle, I stopped to persuade myself that I should investigate whether or not the car worked. I could *drive* to that town! I cajoled. It would be worth whatever disgust, whatever revulsion I sustained from sitting on his seat.

In the end, I just couldn't do it. I just had to keep walking.

16

FOUR OF THEM without their fifth maundered in
a condition of lostness through the wind-maze's
crannies and contours. Navigating the shifty environs,
transitory on the fringes as a choppy sea, the comrades
had but one goal: finding their leader. Meezly, as petite
and unassertive as she was, had formed this merry band
of beleaguered souls unaware that she was so doing.

    The girl was not herself and yet she was the hub
in this circle of friends, the charismatic fulcrum who
balanced their alliance. Loyalty and affection united
them. But she was their adhesive. People like her
were the flames for moths to flutter about and revere.

    Currently they trooped through a wilderness
of diverse wafting cloud shapes. A bunny, a bear,
a rooster. Profiles of people. A sailboat, castle and
choo-choo. Mythical creatures. A unicorn, elephant,
eagle. Monsters and marauders. The variables were
infinite.

    His mind rambling ahead of their feet, Terence
speculated if the magic wand could carve an exit or
zap them out of this scare-scape. Tonka refrained
from testing the notion. What was the use?
They weren't going anywhere at the present.

    "Let us brainstorm to formulate a plan!"
the French wizard rallied.

    "Andale!" hurrahed Terence. He had decided
to speak Spanish instead of barking.

Rhonda said she was planning a new wardrobe in monochromatic tints of cucumber-green. "Either that or something trendy like Farmer Gothic."

"He means a plan to find Meezly," interpreted Juniper.

"Oh, that kind of plan! Gotcha! Anyway, if I were to go Goth, it would have to be something more original than one shade of black," Rhonda yammered. "Like my red ensembles. I bet you didn't know there are about a hundred shades of cherry! Then there's raspberry, strawberry, cranberry, and don't get me started on apple!"

"Callate, muchacha!" Terence wagged a finger instead of a nonexistent tail.

"Oui, we must focus on what matters, which is our missing friend, non?" stated, or asked, Tonka.

The girl apologized. "When I'm nervous I tend to go off on tangents. Of course we need to locate Meezly, so all of us can get out of here and find that pebble or crystal or whatever it is!"

Juniper smiled. "Den we should look in da right place."

The others agreed and the four of them set off, but they didn't get far before a whirlpool of mist expanded around them. They were spindled then flushed through a transparent pipe. A blurred view of menageries, palaces, and fairytale vistas zizzed by.

Meezly's amigos were whumped onto a spongy blue-green mat of pliant mounds. These puffy patches grew at intervals across sandy soil punctuated by upside-down trees with slim brownish-gray trunks and profusions of thin venerable branches like roots. A manicured layer of "grass" — tufts of lime-green needles — formed the leaves.

"Awesome!" Ronnie blurted.

Juniper exclaimed, "Dat is de Dragon Tree! I never seen dem, just in pictures! Dey have resin dat is red. It is called Dragon's Blood."

"Qué suave!" enthused Terence.

"That's so cool," Rhonda grinned. "And it's my favorite color! Maybe I'll keep wearing red."

"Zis place is very curious. Always it is changing!" articulated Tonka.

"Everyding is dat way," cited Juniper. "De life evolves, you know. And we must adapt. But we can also choose de path we wish to follow."

"I don't see a path here," noted Rhonda.

"Dere is always a path."

"Our path leads to Grace," Terence averred.

"Jeez Louise! Her name is Meezly, not Grace! Why do you call her that?" Rhonda gibed.

"Because she's graceful. Everyone has a special name. One they're born with. One they just are."

"Then what's mine?" asked Rhonda.

"Yours is Roja. Spanish for red."

"But I'm not red."

"To me you are."

"Is that a good thing or a bad thing?"

"It's great." Terence grinned.

"Now I'm blushing. Guess I *am* red," laughed Rhonda.

Juniper and Tonka smiled.

A bestial roar caused them all to cringe. Then a clangor resounded, and a guy with a large nose and beard dressed in medieval garb bustled up to them ringing a handbell. "The dragon! The dragon!" he was hollering. "Take cover, fair folk, or it will be your death!"

"Qué lágrima!" Terence yawped.

"Oh, I love dragons!" Ronnie burbled.

"This dragon is not very lovable, miss!" the peasant relayed. "He's big and ornery and nobody likes him!"

As if to illustrate, the beast cruised from
a lavender sky and seized the man in copious jaws.
"See what I meeeeeeean?" His cry faded. Only his
bell remained.

"Wow, that *isn't* very lovable! Or likable!"
Rhonda denounced.

"Use your stick to save him!" urged Juniper to
Tonka.

"I'll try. But it does what it wants." Removing
his hat, the magician withdrew the wand, aimed it and
murmured an improvised spell: "Dragon corruptus!
Wing interruptus!"

Astoundingly, the peasant was released — from
an extreme altitude. They could hark his exclamations
as he landed upon a tree, then bounced onto a cushion
of mossen lumps. The four travelers rushed toward him
and helped the man to his feet.

"My name is Erdwald and I am in your debt,"
he informed them, rubbing his contused posterior.
"You must have brought me luck, for I have not been
eaten this day! Of course, there is always tomorrow."

"Happy to meet you, Erd." Rhonda pumped his
hand. "But it wasn't luck at all."

"I beg to differ, miss. In my humble opinion,
it was most fortunate," protested Erd.

"She means dat our friend is a magic man."
Juniper gestured to an abashed Tonka, who gave
a curt bow. "He saved you!"

"Then I am all the more grateful, dear friends!"
Erd clasped Tonka in an exuberant hug. "I shall tell
the villagers this glorious news!" Retrieving his bell,
he commenced clanging. "A sorcerer has come to rid
us of the dragon!"

No villagers dallied within earshot, but a wyrm's
hearing was very keen. Much like his intellect.

The Dragon, let's call him Girdruff, came barreling back for a skirmish with this sorcerer who had caused him to drop his dinner. At least it wasn't a knight. They were so aggravating with their suits of armor, their blades and shields. A sorcerer should be flaccid, yielding to the bite, less effort.

The rash myth-creant slavered in anticipation, afraid of no man for he was invincible. He hadn't heard the rumors of a legend of a prophecy that a mortal would one day pierce his heart, or he might not have been so cocky.

Gird soared above the fayent forest of Dragon Trees. Although proud to be thusly honored, it didn't prevent him from devouring villagers. Sweeping over the five vassals, he snorted a whiff of fire to show them who was boss.

Erd ceased chiming his bell to cower below a tree. The band of four seekers huddled with him.

"We had no hope until you arrived," the peasant deplored. "Weapons do not penetrate his scales or skin. And we are farmers, not soldiers, in this dell. But there is lore about the hero who can slay him with a sword. It must be you!" He asked Tonka for his autograph.

The magician pulled a signed photo out of his hat. Erdwald thanked him.

"Have you tried a missile?" questioned Terence.

"A missile?" Rhonda slugged his arm. "You would nuke a dragon?"

"Maybe, if it was him or me. But I'd use a plain warhead."

"I don't even know you!" Rhonda shook her head. "Weren't you raised by stray dogs? Didn't you rescue animals from a research lab?"

"Sí. But I was rescued too. I guess I wouldn't harm a dragon, if he were real."

The Dragon

Terence's countenance grew somber as a funeral procession. "But he isn't — he's something wicked. I don't know what. You'll have to take my word for it. When it comes to evil, you've just gotta do what's right."

Juniper exhorted, "We don't need missiles. We have magic!"

"If it works." Tonka was dubious.

"You did save Erd," commended Rhonda.

"Zat I did, young lady. But I was trying to make ze dragon land," the Frenchman confessed.

"Oh."

Erdwald indicated Tonka's wizard wand. "You're going to need to use a sword for the prophecy to come true. If you do one little thing different," he superstitiously cautioned, "the dragon might return!"

"I don't have a sword." Tonka seemed stymied.

"That could be a problem." Erd was nonplussed.

Juniper was practical as ever: "Den you will have to make one! Wid de magic stick!"

"I can try." Experimentally, Tonka angled the rod and hocused, "As steel is poured, fetch forth a sword!"

The wand gave him a pitcher of water.

He pointed the dowel and pocused, "As food is gorged, let blade be forged!"

A basket of grainy brown loaves appeared.

Five stomachs gurgled. Like prisoners, they dined beneath the tree on bread and water.

A rapacious dragon waited on a hilltop. Soon it would be his turn for a banquet.

Tonka gave the matter a final stab: "A sword I need, for a noble deed."

A gleaming longsword vibrated, tip buried in the sand. Tonka walked to it in amazement. He peered down steeped in thought, then stepped away. "I am not ze hero of your tale," he told Erd. "I have my own tale. And I have zis!" He held up his wand.

Erdwald gawked at him with surprise. Solemnly the peasant acceded his destiny and grasped the weapon's haft. He brandished the radiant knightstick dramatically above.

"There's one more teensy-weensy problem," he stated. "I don't know how to use a sword."

"I can teach you," offered Terence.

The others looked at him, eyebrows forming arcs.

"I'm a genius," he shrugged. "I read a book!"

The erudite lad tutored the farmer on expert swordsmanship.

After an hour of training, the squire was knighted and Tonka zapped him into a suit of armor and chainmail.

That is, he zapped him into a pinstripe suit. Then a striped prison suit. Then a gray flannel suit. Then an astronaut suit. Eventually the magician came up with an incantation that produced the desired result, and Sir Erdwald The Excellent was christened.

"Oh, one more tiny thing," he mentioned. "The dragon cannot be killed by an ordinary sword. Unless the blade is as magical as your rod, this was all for nothing. I will confront the dragon and be toast."

It was a dilemma, they all agreed.

The dragon was highly entertained by these preparations. Except for the armor and such. He watched from his hill as the challenger was instructed and dressed and encouraged. Just when he thought the fatuous lout would be sent into battle, there was another delay!

Juniper whispered an idea to the magic man. "I'll try," he pledged.

Tonka waved his wand at one of the upside-down trees. "Dragon's Blood through bark and vein, let this become the creature's bane!"

Dragon Blood Tree

Energy transfused from the baton to the tree, which briefly glowed. "I zink it is done," said Tonka. "At least, somezing happened."

"How can we know for certain?" asked Erd.

"Zere is no ozer way but to try!" the magician forlorned.

Erdwald The Excellent gallantly lowered his helmet's visor and unsheathed his sword. Marching to the enchanted Dragon Tree, the knight was about to swing his blade.

"Hold that thought!" Rhonda interjected. And zipped to embrace the trunk.

"I'm a tree hugger," she defended. "I told the tree what we need and voilà!" She showed them a knot on the smooth bark where a bright red sap had begun to exude.

Courteously bobbing, Erd dipped his sword tip into the rich resin. He bowed at his companions then trekked off, praying the Dragon's Blood had enriched his blade.

Gird, with his acute ears, picked up on the scheme. Launching himself aloft, he swooped inside the valley to belch a firestorm and incinerate the forest to ashes. An orange sea licked from tree to tree until all of them were in flames.

The wyrm reserved a final blast of heat for the knight, to fry him where he stood. Girdruff misjudged the sword's great length, for the sap-enforced blade was rammed up into his chest — hewing through the breastplate that guarded a black heart.

Erdwald and friends watched the beast's flight falter, then spiral out of control. The creature plunged like a payload onto a burning tree and exploded.

Villagers, unseen till that moment, sprang as if from hiding to rollick and lark.

Bidding farewell to the dragon-slayer, four wanderers resumed their lateral journey of finding the forward path of their missing member in search of a stone.

17

I MUST'VE WALKED A MILE since the road to the cabin. My feet were sore, my legs stiff. I hadn't exercised that much in the past year and was sadly out of condition. Grief will do that to a person. It's like a predatory hunter, pillaging energy and stamina like flesh and muscle!

Hardly a cheerful frame of mind to have when surrounded by forest, but I was weak and unfit for the grueling demands of an adventure — any adventure — let alone an overblown survival ordeal that was leading me beyond the parameters of credulity, through the crumpled pages of some crazed horror author's head!

I wished I could curl up in a nice soft bed under a pile of warm blankets. I had left home to track down a stone that might be cursed. Instead, all I could think about was being comfortable again. It seemed like such a luxury, hobbling along a highway dampened by off-and-on showers, my stomach empty and aching, mouth dry. I'm sure you're thinking, *Why didn't she glug down some of that rain when she had the chance?* I did, although it wasn't my intention. I was kind of disconcerted by attempting to stay alive.

And then I realized that I needed to use the bathroom an hour ago or three, but of course there was no facility when I needed it. I really had to go! It's always worse when you're cold. I wished I had thought of it earlier, while I was in that cabin for example, but I wasn't about to return there now!

I didn't see any rest-stop signs. My only choice was to enter the woods far enough to not be visible from the road.

The deeper I went in this frightmare, feeling like I had been chipped of ice, the tougher it was to quell my nerves. I shuddered from a chill that frosted out of my bones, a frigidness that was more than the air's caress. It emanated from shock and terror.

Teeth clacking, my body spastic, I trepidly stepped off the side of the highway and roved like a lost lamb toward the edge of the timber.

If it was dark along the highway, it was a thousand times blacker within the trees. And I was not inclined to be brave having met two monsters, no less, in this neck of the woods. My optimism was pretty impaired.

As for nature skills, I had never traveled to those extraneous reaches in search of antiquities with my parents. Never camped in a forest or even my backyard. I did pretend to camp in the den one night. I fantasized it was the cave of a cute fluffy bear.

This was no fantasy, no sweet children's tale or playtime romp. I couldn't wake up from it like a bad dream. It would be here until I dealt with the reality or died. Either way, I was on my own.

My loafers were a disaster, yet I was still preoccupied avoiding the spread of a prodigious puddle over an expanse of dry ground sheltered from the storm by dense boughs. I had chosen level terrain whereas I should have selected a basin, a shallow depression. Live and learn. Not that I planned to be in a similar situation ever again!

As I was focused at the ground, I heard a snap — the kind of noise you could go your life without hearing and be content. The kind of sound that could make you lose your mind for just a minute out of irrational (or was it?) fear. I quickly glanced around, feeling vulnerable.

Completing my business, paranoia heightening, I hasted toward the perimeter of the trees.

And suddenly had to halt in confusion.

It wasn't where I left it. Where my sense of direction mandated the forest line should be! What was going on? This wasn't right. The woods had shifted. Trees don't do that. They have roots, anchors, deeply embedded in the soil. They can't just get up and move!

Strange as it seemed, that's what happened. There seemed no other explanation. The trees moved.

"Okay. This is really getting weird," I said aloud, for the sake of argument. For the sake of maintaining my grip. The forest had adjusted itself and I was lost. This bothered me more than the monsters; insulted my intelligence or something to that effect. The truth was, I was terrified of losing the highway, my sole connection to my friends and my world. Whether it was a wormhole, just a link, or my salvation — I had to get back to it somehow!

The woodlings stood murky and nondescript. I stood among them and turned my head, scouting. There were no landmarks, nothing I could use to regain my bearings.

That gave me a notion. I garnered a branch from the needled floor and placed it in a circumspect position, lodged in the crook of a tree limb and trunk. Aligning myself to the stick, I could use it as a guide, forage every direction, not missing any possible route thanks to the branch. I would find the highway. Unless that, too, had moved!

I began my explorations, having forgotten about the snapping sound; perhaps attributing it to the rearrangement.

Presently, I was forced to conclude that the turnpike must have shifted like the trees. I was hopelessly lost.

A branch cracked. I bated my breath as if to
hide by standing still. There was an odious vibe,
the queasiness of dread, cramping my belly and chest.

Brush rattled. Then I could distinctly identify
the strong thrashing surge of a body charging straight
to where I grimaced. Like a rabbit I fled, fatigued yet
adrenaline-fueled. My pursuer crashed after me —
by the sound of it, as large as a moose or bear.

On a sun-drenched sward I twisted an ankle and
hit damp ground with my hands and knees. Out of the
undergrowth roared a small furry beast. I was being
chased by a weasel.

The elongated reddish mammal had a white
stomach, long neck, and comically abbreviated legs.
Plowing into the glade like a whimsical character
Lewis Carroll might have invented, he launched himself
in a hissy-fit: spine arched, his tail bushed, jumping to
the side, hopping backwards in a peculiar sort of dance.
I expected him to talk, but when he saw that I was too
jumbo for a meal, the creature turned tail and split.

Snippets of laughter fluctuated.

My ears perked, thinking I might not be alone.

There came a second jocular peal, weaving through
the pines then gone.

"Hello? Is anyone there?"

My queries echoed, reverberated trunk to trunk.

"I'm lost, can you help me?" I pleaded.

A chorus of giggles responded. Not the antics of
children. A profligate fermentious ballyhoo.

Bass intonations. Then a banshee wind soughed.

"Who's there?" My voice was hoarse, my calls
unanswered. A shadow dodged my gaze. Elusive figures
darted. Vegetation crinkled. I felt a lurch inside my
brain, a dizziness. I was coming unraveled, I diagnosed.
Profoundly distressed. I was imagining things. Maybe
all of it had been the figments of a fragmented mind.
I would have liked to believe that.

Better to be crazy than to actually be in a situation so hazardous and beyond your control that it could drive you insane! From the laughs and movements, it was almost as if I were being menaced by a group, not an individual. I perceived they were all around, watching me, taunting. But who were they? *Where* were they? All I saw was trees. And then it struck me that it *was* the trees!

Once I knew what to look for, I began to filter out the doubts and prejudices that hamper us from viewing what isn't natural or logical: the paranormal plane inhabited by the spirits of the forest. I detected their subtleties, their nuances. The furtive and sly alterations.

As my vision became clearer, I discerned that the trees could sneak about, retract their roots then bury them with ease. It was a devilish surprise. Who knew? All this time we thought they were inferior, stagnant, a resource to be exploited — hacked and sawed, stripped and honed, chewed up to pulp. Charred to the ground through carelessness. We did not regard them as having spirits, or even as life. We did not respect that a forest is a culture, a web of intricate relationships; a living breathing entity. Humans gave trees the privilege of bearing our words and tales whether noble or crass. But we did not grant them the reverence and gratitude they deserved. We did not aspire to co-exist in harmony, we simply conquered and divided. Or perhaps they wouldn't have been so angry.

Although I was no tree hugger like Rhonda, I thought woods to be alluring and tranquil. I preferred them from a distance, like the rain: on the tube, in a movie or photograph. I was not an outdoors person. It took four walls and a roof to make me feel at home.

This night I was exposed to the wild untamed heart of Nature. The raw violent side that dated back to the beginning of primeval history. I was in the thick of it, and I was being held accountable.

I'm not saying that I wasn't responsible to a degree. I used timber products. I lived in a wood-based society.

But the trees wanted to make an example of me, to vent their rage and exact revenge. Layers of tree rings circled me in contrary motions, surrounding, dancing like a cult of pagan moon worshippers. It was dizzying — amplified by the mocking trills of birds on their boughs, who seemed just as irate and bigoted.

I felt helpless against the odds of a forest versus me. I couldn't find my way out, much less oppose an entire woodland community!

My nose is seldom, if ever, mistaken. It had been signalling by being itchy that I should stay out of the trees since before I impetuously stepped in. Now it was making me sneeze, the way someone will do with an allergic reaction. My intuition began flashing too, bells and sirens.

The trees quit dancing. The earth shook as something separated from its berth in a hillside. The hulking goliath, more than a dozen feet tall, clothed in bark and foliage, clomped towards me. Eyes blazing, a masculine aspect set in a scowl, vines and leaves comprising his locks and beard, the king of the treedom stooped to inspect me.

"Who are you?" he boomed.

"Arletta Trimble." I thought I'd best be formal.

"Why are you here?" he rumbled.

"That's a very good question," I cheerily acknowledged. "I've been wondering it myself. I was supposed to be on a treasure hunt to find a stone. Instead I got swallowed by a storm and spat out on Highway Zero! I was about to bust my bladder so I made a pit-stop in the woods."

"Homo Sapiens are all alike! You rob our minerals, chop us down, hunt our friends and defile our home!" criticized the bearded tree lord. His wide features ducked closer.

I was a little grossed that vines coiled from his nostrils and mouth.

"Does this look like a toilet to you?" he gruffed.

I sheepishly mumbled, "Well, no. But don't the animals have to use it too?"

"This is their home! You do not belong. You left the forest, built your cities. But still you come back to take what is not yours!" The green giant brooded sternly. "Your kind has shamelessly dirtied the air and water. You take the beauty of the forest, the land, and twist it into ugliness — constructing machines to erect your ever-higher towers, defacing the splendor of the earth!"

"Since you put it that way, it does seem sort of bad," I admitted. Though I was also thinking, *Like I really need this now!* A lecture on saving the planet, when I was in the "muddle" of trying to save myself from an escalating thrill-jaunt through a gauntlet of hair-raising crises!

"There is no excuse!" the big guy proclaimed, pounding a great fist on the floor of the glade. He had quite a temper.

"I'm sorry, Mister, uh . . ." I hesitated. We hadn't been introduced.

"Your people call me Green Man. I call myself Uthwah. It is a name older than these hills," the forest king stated.

"Hey, I've heard of you!" I grinned. "It's very nice to meet you, Mister Green. Mister Man. Mister Green Man"

"Where is the stone you seek?" An impatient growl.

"I wish I knew. It would sure make finding it a lot easier," I lamely jested.

Green Man did not have a sense of humor. Just when I thought we had established a rapport, he divulged that sacrificing me wouldn't heal the many wounds — but it could serve as a warning to the human race.

That's when I remembered my bag of tricks.
As I was being ushered to the oldest tree in the forest,
I casually tucked a hand into the canvas sack.

This better be good, I thought. But I had no idea
what might help me get out of this bind. I was hoping
the bag knew.

My fingers found nothing unusual, nothing
I hadn't put there myself. I considered another awkward
hectic flight but what was the use? I'd be tripped and
bamboozled by the devious nature of Nature. Not that
you can't trust Mother Nature. But you should never
try to fool her. Or fool *with* her.

I cogitated whether Mother Nature was Green Man's
mommy.

Or did they share a romantic bond? His girlfriend?
His wife? I wondered if it was impolite to ask.

Keeping my hand inside the bag, in case it was
merely having trouble to decide, I posed before my
punisher.

The Elder had a broad rutted trunk mottled with
a hodgepodge of lichens, peppered by globules of black
mildew. There seemed a patina of disapproval about
him, telegraphed in the fissures of his graying bark and
the slouch of his boughs. His leaves were sparse, hearing
dim. Green Man ramped his voice to a thunderous octave
so the aged spirit could get the gist . . . how I was to be
martyred as reparation for the sins of my species. I didn't
point out the flaws in this plan, such as the fact that none
of my species were likely to even get wind of my execution.
And that if they did by some flukish revelation, they
probably wouldn't care — except for the few who knew
me.

Oldie Moldy, creaking and groaning, summoned
his roots out of the soil. He wrapped the snaking tubes
around my torso. Blunt tips burrowed, drilling with feeble
vigor to absorb the liquids that primarily constituted my
innards.

The assailment was reminiscent of the rutabogey in the cemetery. These woods crawled with bloodthirsty beings! I would never look at a tree the same.

Out of the blue, the hand in my bag was holding a hatchet. Okay! I'd still be surrounded, but I'd go down swinging.

That was the thing about me, what could prove a fatal shortcoming: I was fearless. I don't mean I was never afraid. I was what you could call a worrywart. When I had to, though, I stood up for myself.

Drawing the weapon, I proceeded to hack me some roots. My executioner squelped like a run-over rat. Chopping until I was free, I brandished the tomahawk in an intimidating fashion and backed my way away.

But where was I to go? Everywhere I turned there were more of them — firm, statuesque, flexing their limbs — and these had fresher sap in their veins. I would not get far. Nor did I have any hope of emerging from their treacherous cabal.

And then a truly strange thing transpired. Stranger than anything else I had thus encountered on that windswept eve. I felt a warmth flow from the hatchet to my hand; up my arm into my bosom. The tool had vanished, as if smelted into this golden heat which streamed like honey throughout my body. I shrank, while simultaneously endowed by peace and confidence, enveloped by a sparkling aura. I floated to the air as if I were a fairy.

The trees could only swat their great branches in vexation.

Flooded with rapture, waving farewell to my adversaries, I began to drift upwards. Green Man, eyebrows knit crossly, attempted to gouge my magic bubble with a well-aimed forefinger.

The shimmering orb lofted beyond his reach. And coltishly evaded the pokes of twigs from higher boughs that swiped at my ethereal carriage.

Not to be outdone, the titan sicced a hawk.
His bird's beak ruptured the gauzy sphere. My aura
dissipated yet I didn't fall. I had become. Shucked
of my cocoon, double wings spread and I sailed past
Green Man's gaze — where I caught my reflection,
a dainty green lacewing.

Above the forest, I promptly scoped the ribbon
of road and gently touched down upon its shoulder.
Personifying, unshrinking, I continued my journey
where it had left off: eleven miles to the nearest
town.

18

GOURD'S SENSE OF GUILT — that palpable onus
he toted around like a hump on his spine — had been
tweaked by the gaggle of children and beasts. He had
borne with him for decades the weight of the lives his
actions cost. Every war of any duration accrued
collateral damage. By bomb or bullet, as expendable
pawns, innocents were cut down. How could a decent
man ever justify to himself or balance that he might
have been culpable? With what words could he convince
the souls of those victims, and their families, that it was
necessary; an acceptable loss?

Grief knew nothing of causes and greater goods.
Those were mere ideals and perspectives. Sorrow was
a deep chasm, with a rickety rope bridge spanning its
crags. He hadn't been able to tread beyond the abyss.
He was frozen above, at the distance where he had
come too far to turn back, and it was still too far across.

He now felt overwhelmed. Whatever inadequate
excuses he had made to himself to get through each
day, to stare at himself in the mirror, had evaporated.
Sinking to his knees, he buried his face in figurative
bloodied hands. His body convulsed. The heart of him
throbbed with anguish. His face furrowed with shame.
And yet he could not weep.

He thought he had shut off his emotions like
a valve. Thought he was hardened enough to withstand
anything that came and persevere, do what had to be
done. He thought he had left his scruples back on the
battlefield.

War was a machine of enormous pulleys and gigantic gears with megalodonic teeth that could rend and grind the bodies and minds of men like brittle twigs then spew them out into Society with nothing or little left to give. Too often a veteran was repaid for his service, for his sacrifices and risks and losses, by indifference. Rejection. Being chucked on the street because he didn't fit in. Because he was changed by that machine — broken and gnawed and disfigured — and the pieces could never be put back again the way they were when he was young and whole.

Richard Gourd was such a man. Such a misfit. He had no life left, other than the shards that had been pasted and patched together in some semblance of humanity by medics and shrinks and chaplains and fellow survivors — before they died of neglect or cancer; alcoholism, overdose, or some other self-inflicted wound.

What brought him to this state was not a single day but many wretched days. And yet there was the worst, the vilest, out of a profusion of severe and darkest days that stayed with him no matter what. Always tinging the recesses of his mind with unimaginable thoughts.

He had been a soldier. Not a man in uniform, but a fighting machine. He obeyed commands, followed the orders of superiors, because that was what a soldier did. What he had been recruited, trained, and programmed for.

Now and then a soldier had to think for himself. Had to pretend he was still a man deep down where the soul was believed to reside. The day he shot his best friend had been such a day. He had been forced to choose, and it would haunt him ever after.

They were on their own, thinking for themselves, in a situation that was off the record. There would be no report filed in a neat manila folder. It wasn't protocol so it wasn't official, wasn't sanctioned or condoned by the powers-that-be, the high mucky-mucks.

This patrol never existed. And then, when
a well-intentioned act went haywire, it was hushed up.

"Sometimes what the brass don't know won't hurt
nobody." That's what his friend Mason said when Gourd
stumbled across the civilians who needed help.

Families, that's all they were. That's all it ever
was, any town in any land. What the whole world of
humankind came down to in a nutshell: just a bunch
of families. That's how each man began and ended.
Unless he was never wanted. Unless he went out
alone.

That's how it was for Mason, the man of
one name, who didn't know if it was his first or last.
And for Richard Gourd. They shared that much,
two misbegotten guys who never had a home.
Who never knew a mother's love. A father's pride.
A brother or sister. It made them who they were.
For better or worse. It changed them from who they
might have been.

Like anything that transpires in the life of a child
that shouldn't or mightn't have happened but did.
That could have been different, could have been better.
That wasn't asked for, wasn't deserved, it just was.

That day, the regrets of a boy had surfaced in the
mind of a man as he studied those families. They had
their own uphevalent stories. Struggling to stay alive
in occupied territory, their everyday world reduced to
the ashes and dust of War. It wasn't easy, whatever
side of the fence they were from.

He felt for them, back when he still could; read
the fear in their eyes, as stark as the gutted windows
of the building where they had taken refuge.

Gourd and Mason were assigned to seek out the
enemy. They were not supposed to deviate from orders.
It was never their responsibility to save the last residents
of a village. In this one they found a massacre.

Nothing new; civilian casualties were a lot more common than folks back home could be aware. It was the big secret, how it wasn't just between armies. It was messy and spilled over. The Nazi war criminals weren't the only ones to target the defenseless. It happened far more than people liked to realize, just as heinous abuses occurred in their neighborhoods behind closed doors. Secrets made it all easier to swallow, easier to ignore. Because it would drive them insane to know everything that was really going on in the world.

With the advent of news crews and documentary cameras in the field, these truths became more difficult to conceal. That's part of why some activities were off the books. Less red tape and bureaucrats. Fewer hotheads griping about rights and wrongs.

This patrol was Black Ops because there was a tip the other side was using the tiny village. Intel didn't say what for. Aerial footage was inconclusive. It was a reconnaissance mission and might violate civilian authority. That was what they were told. It couldn't have been farther from what they found.

Carnage was everywhere. But not in the streets. Bodies were propped in chairs, lain on beds inside the homes. Two families had escaped, alerted by a cut-off scream. They were cached in a workshop behind sheets of metal propped as a fake wall. A child's whimper led Gourd to their hideout.

He knew a smattering of the dialect. Combined with gestures, he deduced that someone or something had murdered the rest of their community during the night like a phantom wind. They were scared, suffering from shock. They still feared the monster would return.

Richard sent Mason to find a truck or van large enough to transport them.

Gourd tried to comfort the locals. It took awhile. Females and children were sobbing. The men were pale and silent, with tears in their eyes.

An engine sounded outside then stopped. Gourd had his hands full calming a wave of panic. Mason gradually came in, and the soldiers led the group out to a light-blue van that looked pretty worn. The windshield and side windows were missing. The tires had no tread. But it should get them out of this fly-infested hellhole.

Gourd sought to escort the civilians to the closest town and leave them at its outskirts. The mission was accomplished. The village was clear; no enemies. Just a bunch of frightened people to get to safety, then they would report back to their camp.

He moved to climb into the driver's seat of the van. Mason halted him with a hand on his arm. "Let them drive." It almost sounded like a warning. His eyes had a funny look.

"I want to get them there in one piece," Richard told him. "In case we're attacked along the route, I'll drive this. You take the other vehicle and lead the way."

"That isn't what I had in mind," argued Mason. It was a plea.

Gourd shrugged it off, couldn't think what was unthinkable, though he would blame himself for not suspecting until it was too late. He slammed the driver's door, cranked the starter. An explosion, rigged toward the back, pitched him through the vacant windshield.

Stunned, his neck and shoulder bleeding, Gourd picked himself up and gaped at the flaming automobile. It was too late to save them.

"Shame. Must have been booby-trapped," Mason remarked. Something about his tone and expression . . .

Gourd's mind flashed with the fact that Mason had demolition skill, that the two friends had gone through explosives instruction together, along with combat training. That his buddy had access to the vehicle and had disappeared the night before, giving an excuse that didn't hold water.

"Was it you?" Richard asked in disbelief.

With a sad smile, Mason shifted both hands to his rifle. "You don't have to say anything. I snapped. Maybe it's Battle Fatigue. I'll get over it. Others do. We'll swear an oath like we used to — we're Blood Brothers, remember?"

They had saved each other countless times. Wanting to save Mason now, Richard shook his head. "Don't," he begged as his right hand tightened on his weapon.

"Come on, man, you wouldn't. It doesn't have to be like this." Appealing with his eyes, then accepting, Mason brought his gun up.

Gourd fired. Bullets impacted his best friend's torso. Mason's bullets strafed Richard's helmet and his uninjured shoulder. They fell in unison. One got up.

Mason briefly stood over his buddy. "You shouldn't have done that, *pal.*" He spat out the final word.

The military vehicle roared away. Gourd closed his eyes. It was the last time he cried.

Wreckage was sighted in a ravine from the air. Mason had lost control of the wheel.

Gourd lost the ability to feel, to forgive. He would carry with him daily the guilt and horror of killing the families as well as his best friend. He had devoted himself to repaying these debts.

And yet sensations stirred from abeyant slumber like a Grizzly with a growling stomach . . . As did a regiment of Civil War skeletons in disheveled blue and gray uniforms, flesh disintegrated, bones clanking and clinking while they rose to their feet. Gourd's eyes bulged, then blurred from a nostalgic montage: the memory of baking bread; the wind in the willows; a cozy warm bed; a giggling brook and the laughter of children. He blinked.

The corps of spirited cadavers ranged around him, grinning with surly unlipped mirth as they hoisted bayonets.

Civil War Skeletons

Gourd considered drawing his handgun, but figured he wasn't that great a shot and would probably hit more gaps than bones. Besides, there were too many of them and he was surrounded.

The clunkheads diverged into ragtag inimical factions, rehashing History, allegorical hatchets unburied. Generations-old discord seemed very much alive beyond the grave.

The soldier of any war, sent back to the mundane world, must amble a shade apart — a reincarnation virtually invisible, eyes forever maimed, grappling with a leviathan of hindsight. Those who died fighting went down as heroes in the eyes of comrades, yet awoke in their version of Valhalla with skulls barren, apprehending nothing from the trials. They too were modified. Trapped in an endless parade of scars.

Hollow sockets glared, choosing sides. North versus South, despite holesome uniforms being practically identical, the way twins might dress. Motivated by the residue of their last thought, to decimate the enemy, knobsters reconvened the conflict where it left off. Out of lead balls and bullets, they rushed like emotions. Pronged musket muzzles clashed in a klutzily choreographed swordfight. Richard Gourd found himself between the cutting edges of a Light Brigade re-enactment. A gonzo ginsu slice-and-dice blade run.

He was about to become chopped liver and other assorted organs when the floor sundered and he descended to a substratum of the cloudy turmoil.

Tromping through the cellar of the storm, the frazzled veteran berated himself for losing track of the three violence-prone individuals he had opted to keep tabs on while detoured from his undercover duty as a cop. He also wished he was still following the girl who they were following, to protect her from them and the other dangers here.

Wherever this was, wherever they were, he wasn't doing any good by roaming off in solitude to lick his wounds like a whipped pup.

Steeling his jaw, Richard Gourd vowed to locate that gal and keep her from harm.

19

A MILE DOWN there was a gravel lane into the trees. You can imagine what went through my head: Another road, another monster? An additional chance to be hoodwinked by those crafty woodsmen? Or an innocent opportunity to find help? "Okay, I'll bite," I murmured. And ventured along the trail, which was only capacious enough for a vehicle going one way. Did that mean you could drive in but you couldn't drive out?

Wind was picking up, howling as if it had a soul and a voice and was angry about something — shaking a mighty fist. I still believed, in spite of all I'd been through on this day, that such things were purely fiction. Basically, I thought I would wake up in my bed after one fruitcake of a dream, eat a dish of Fruit Loops for breakfast, and get on with my life.

I was so naïve.

If something stares you in the face, wags its tongue at you, conks you on the bean, and you still insist it isn't there . . . you have a serious case of plausible deniability. Or you're out of touch with reality.

I don't know what my problem was.

Oh yeah. I was so naïve.

What I wasn't was born yesterday. Yet I still, after all that was said and done up to this chapter in my life, took a hike on that road into *those* woods! Looking back, I can't explain it.

Obviously I survived. You know that because you're reading this.

Unless I died and came back as a horror author. Or returned as a ghost to possess someone's body to type the book for me.

I guess you can't be sure.

What you can know for certain is that something terrible waited for me at the end of that road.

Appropriately as I crunched along the gravel, a chill lanced through me and I shivered. White pebbles began to rain, blending with the path of stones laid out before me. There must have been a moon although I couldn't see it. I could see the chunks of hail bounce and roll. I could view my breath hang on the air like mist. I could not foretell the future. I did not have psychic visions. I had a nose for trouble, a nose that was currently ice-cold. But a nose cannot see. If it could, I would never have set foot on that isolated lane.

It seemed I was wet more often than dry. The hail subsided to a monsoonish torrent. I don't like getting wet, which meant I was miserable.

The tree line loomed as a diabolic threshold that I was loath to traverse. But I was weary, my feet chafed, so I limped over into the woods. I needed to find my friends. I didn't care about the stone at that moment. I just wanted to go home. And home was not along this highway.

My brain vacillated from believing I was back in the normal world, with rules and physics, to outlandishly conceiving that I had breached the barrier between Real and Unreal and was stuck somewhere in a netherous gulf of nowhereland. The stomping ground of grotesqueries and mythicks, in which nothing was ever sacred or what it seemed, and everything was never what it should be or shouldn't.

You can see how discombobulated I felt.

As the trees encompassed me — probably closing in behind but I didn't dare peek — half of me abandoned all hope of making it out alive.

The other half, the optimistic side, thought it was a long-shot.

I could feel the animosity of the pines; the willows and oaks, birches and maples; the spruces and cedars. Could hear them bristle; the agitation of leaves and needles, acorns and cones. Every tree in that forest was against me. Yet they permitted me to pass. Did they know something?

Rain ceased, coming and going for no reason.

I decided to whistle walking towards my doom, then couldn't determine whether it should be a happy or sad song, Rock or Blues, uplifting Dixieland Jazz or a moody dirge. Finally I picked a violin concerto.

That's when I caught a glimmer of the lake in the moonlight. Silver crystals slow-danced on the waves, cobbling an avenue of dimples and ridges. It was magnificent. I forgot about whistling, which was a good thing. I'm a lousy whistler. And I had no idea how to whistle like a violin.

I tramped to the water, glad I didn't miss the wonder of this secret cove. And *that's* when I gandered the lakehouse. It was a cottage built on the shore. There were no lights and yet it looked so ordinary and safe, so civilized, I was just in awe.

After what I had been through, I was triple shy and approached the mysterious abode with paramount bias. Climbing onto the porch, I rapped at a screen-door. Of course there would be no answer. But then again, maybe there would. And maybe I wouldn't want to be there when it happened.

Well, as it happened, nothing happened. The door went unanswered so I went inside. What else was I going to do? It's only breaking and entering when you break something, right?

Besides, I would have gladly been arrested to get out of that waking nightmare!

Static electricity flickered. Thunder resonated, too loud for comfort.

I found the doors unlocked. At first I was pleased. This was going to be easy. I use the phone, raid the fridge, leave a note thanking the owners for their hospitality. Piece of cake! Actually, I was hoping to find cake. A tasty Crumb Cake. A Coffeecake. An Angel's Food or Pineapple Upside-Down.

I quickly forgot about cake.

Stepping into that house was one of the worst mistakes I would ever make. I kid you not. It was literally a chamber of horrors!

To begin with, there was blood. Red handprints decorated the walls; maroon footprints tracked the hardwood floors, as if the former occupant had been finger-and-toe-painting.

Then I beheld the severed body parts, descrying a hand and foot by gruesome surprise in the refrigerator. They were the only things in there, to my dismay, and had been utilized artistically. But the coats of rusty dried crud were no brand of oil paint or tempera.

Picasso's other pieces of human jigsaw puzzles were hidden with more cunning flair. An entire person tipped out on me when I opened a closet, for instance. The corpse was a conglomeration of different victims sewn and glued and stapled and duct-taped together. The image will stay with me. What type of mentality is capable of doing such things?

I wasn't anxious to find out.

The bedroom was decorated by human heads mounted on the walls "featuring" an array of contrived bizarre expressions.

The washing machine contained clothes that were still being worn. I slammed the lid down and nearly blacked out. I had to crouch, hugging myself, dizzy and ill.

When the sickness passed, I just wanted to escape.
I didn't care to examine further "masterpieces". That
was a job for the police.

Rain drummed the roof. Thunder bowled a strike.

"A phone, a phone," I muttered. I would have to
search. The dwelling was spartan, few furnishings.
I wasn't sure anyone lived there. And if they did, they
didn't anymore. They were dead.

Horrified out of my wits, I squeamishly combed
the house without really looking as I peevishly scolded
Providence that this wasn't too good for my anxiety!
My eyes were unfocused, my stare indirect. I breathed
sparingly to obviate the stench. And distinguished
things that made my flesh crawl. I did not find
a telephone. The cottage was vacant other than
the deceased and dismembered crammed in the
appliances.

Exiting a gritty crime scene, my heart fibrillating
like mad, stomach nauseated, I shambled sickly along
the water's edge in the downpour. Whoever had made
the bungalow a lair might be back any minute. If it was
a who. I had seen plenty of *whats* in these woods and,
dream or not, I had no alternative but to contend with
the next freak in line if I hung around here. I should
have stayed on the highway. Better still, I should have
stayed in bed this morning!

That methodology, however, wouldn't get me
through life.

The rain halted as if a sign. Was the omen
positive or negative? My nose twitched like an eel
that was electrocuting itself. I should have listened.

Turning to retrace my steps on the access road,
I was petrified by panic. What if the perpetrator was
already coming? What if I ran straight into the fiend
on that gravel lane?

Either I had to risk a face-to-face meeting with one foe, or I could follow the road surreptitiously through the trees and risk a platoon of enemies there.

While I was fixated on the route, water splashed behind me in the lake. I figured, just a fish jumping. Nothing to worry about. Except the sound kept repeating. And getting closer. I realized that something was coming, all right, but not from the road!

Spinning with a strangled cry, heart banging wildly, I boggled at an immense pellucid creature seeping out of the drink. This lake monster was not your typical plesiosaur of legend but a shapeless transparency, an amoebic organism, electricity sparking within its composition.

The jelly slimeball changed after contacting air — from a veined amorphous blob to an amphibious gray man-beast with catfish tentacles around his mouth, crimson eyes, webbed hands and feet, and a paunchy ribbed torso. The fish fellow would've made me laugh, like a B-movie throwback you'd like to toss back for being too cheesy, only this monster had a mouthful of foul jagged teeth. And an arrantly sadistic disposition.

Judging by his handiwork in the house, it was evident he wasn't killing for food like most beasts. Nor out of vindictive sentiment like a human psycho might do. The brute, driven by a baser instinct, a berserk villainy, was murdering for sport.

That knowledge sufficed to scare the daylights out of me. I did not wish to become one of his specimens to dissect and sculpt; a mere implement to paint with. I felt my life had too much merit to be cut off like a moribund appendage and displayed on a shelf.

As the cretin grabbed for me, I raced toward an old rowboat espied by the house. Pushing the vessel down the bank, I jumped inside and shoved away from the shore with an oar.

The Lake Monster

You have to understand, I was pretty frightened. I could imagine myself being added to his macabre collection. That was incentive enough to take radical measures. I should have known he could swim. He was a lake monster! He had emerged from the cove!

So there I was, placing myself at a disadvantage; playing right into his slick webbed mitts. The boat had just one oar, which I had to use as a paddle. And the bottom was leaking. My shoes were swiftly submerged. "Oh man, this isn't good!" I exclaimed. How long would the skiff stay afloat? And where was I hoping to go that the monster couldn't get to first?

Paddling inanely, my actions inept, I steered for the middle of the lake — where my plight would be all the worse. Unlike the monster, I wasn't an agile swimmer. I wasn't at home in the water. Navigating to the deepest part of the lake was about the daftest thing I could have done. So of course, that's what I did.

As I am also wont to do, I had to ponder at a time when I should have been concerned with more important matters — like how to survive — whereof this creature originated. Was it a fugitive demon from the inferno, or some random mutation? Did a spaceship or meteor land in the lake, ferrying the beast from another galaxy?

My vessel was filling up fast. And then I lost the oar. Not that it was my fault. The paddle was wrested out of my hands, a clever ploy. The brute had stranded me. Even if I could swim well, I would be no match for him in the water.

Then I recalled the bag, its abilities. I wasn't defenseless. Would it save me this time? Was there a limit? Had I used my three wishes?

Before I could check, the monster's head splurged from the lake beside the boat. He grabbed the rim and pulled. I threw my weight the opposite. It wouldn't take much to tug the skiff down.

To be honest, I didn't see any way out of the deed and thought I was a goner. But then he quit his attempt to sink the craft and towed it instead. We were coasting to shore, to a small pier by the house.

Perhaps he wanted me alive. Perhaps torture was part of his game.

I jammed my hand inside the blue sack. "Come on, once more!" I fidgetously begged. My hand was empty. I discovered no miracle object, and no warmth infused my arm. *Please!*

The boat bumped the pier, and the monster tied a rope at the bow to a stanchion then waded from the water. He splatted across planks to drag me out of the skiff. I resisted, kicking as he bore me to the cottage without emotion, his visage implacable.

The gray ghoul conveyed me to a room where he had arranged a workshop, replete with the gore-encrusted instruments of his hobby. The ogre flopped me onto a blood-stained table and fastened ankle restraints. As he cuffed my left wrist, my right hand dove to the bag for a final bid prior to being shackled.

My fist clenched an abrasive white dust, which I flung into the beast's eyes. Howling, he plucked a sickle from a tool-rack. My bag overflowed with salt. I threw a palmful at his face. Screaming, the beast was repelled as he was about to slice me down the center like a coroner. His flesh blistered in reaction.

Freeing my left hand, I gripped the bag with both, folding back the flap. When he came towards me again, I spilled more salt on his wounds. The creature was thwarted, tumbling and writhing on the floor. I mercilessly unloaded the bag over him, including a jumble of personal belongings.

The lake monster withered, drying and shriveling like a snail.

Oh man! I slid from the table, the bag strapped to me, after liberating my legs. I didn't bother retrieving any of my stuff.

Tree branches raked my face and clothes as I fled down the lane. A fomentous wind blew, exciting a flurry of leaves and twigs. My side soon hurt, and my legs were like cement. I had skittered out of another surreal predicament. Another phantasmagoric tight corner.

I did not wish to return to Route Zero. It was nothing but trouble. I wanted to wake up, needed to get out of this insaneness. But I surmised that the only direction where that could happen, where it was even remotely possible, was the highway to Woebegone.

20

MINERVA BALEFULLY INDISPUTED that Bozos One and Two had better not impede her plot to heist the jewel, which was her golden ticket out of a rat-nest room in a dilapidated building. She wasn't about to let that ticket fall into the hands of the daffy dodos she was saddled with, thanks to them knowing about the rock too. She had to keep an eye on the dimwits so they wouldn't get to it first — not that she thought they could think their way out of a paper sack, but you couldn't be too careful.

"Speed it up!" she gurred at them, leading the charge on her stubby yet sturdy legs. The three were hustling past a snoring shark-bird with a feathered dorsal fin and a serrated overbite from his underjaw.

Precious little had sunk in since their induction to the zany world. Lacking imagination, they could no more marvel at its wonders than they would a trip to Disneyland.

Spiro didn't appreciate being bossed around by a woman. It reminded him of being nagged by his mother, and he didn't appreciate that just as much! Not that he had been any happier being bossed around by his father. And not that he was that great at making decisions for himself. He didn't like having a boss, period, so that's why he preferred to not have a job. Which was probably why he had put up with his mother. His father was a crook and spent his time serving time. Since childhood Spiro had contemplated a life of crime, but he was afraid of going to jail.

The doctor said he was a late bloomer afraid to leave the flowerbed. Another reason to punch the guy: calling him a flower!

Driscoll was smiling with the usual anti-social dearth of esteem for his dysfunctional playgroup. This day had turned out to be a treat. He was enjoying himself tremendously. The others were even more fun, hardy-har! He snickered, shuffling at the tail-end of the parade of would-be bandits and one complacent smirker. His mind sifted a card catalogue of mayhem he'd like to perform upon the ignoble pair. But he liked this camaraderie, the sense of unity. It was unprecedented to be sure. Even if they served as fodder for his parasitic needs, he was developing a fondness. An affinity. Like a taste for bugs and blood. He had plans for them. And he didn't care to rush.

The cohorts of sorts arrived at an intersection where oddball traffic darted every which way at once. Unicyclers, downhill racers, dogsledders, and a guy with a skateboard for each foot. Jaywalkers, kite-skaters, ice-cream truckers and trikeriders. A bearded biker on a hog (the kind that oinks), and a runaway caboose.

"Don't you think we should ask directions?" piped Spiro as they waited for a lull.

"There isn't time!" yelped Missus Drager, pink-complected. Her blood pressure was elevated. "We have to find the girl, and then we have to rob her if she found the jewel! If she didn't, we have to get her to tell us where it is! And that's a lot to do!" The more she thought about it, the more she needed that rock.

Driscoll laughed. "I don't care about a stupid jewel."

"Then why are you here?" disdained Spiro.

"That's for me to know." Driscoll winked.

Spiro flexed his fists, wanting to pummel the goof — he hated being winked at — but the guy creeped him out.

"Boys, boys, there's enough for us all if we work together," fibbed Minerva, though she had no intention of sharing.

"You can fight over my piece of the pie," Driscoll dismissed. He had other interests.

"That's what you say now." Spiro eyed him narrowly.

The eyebrowless shaver mutely grinned.

Minerva gave them both a disgruntled look. She was tired of hearing there was no jewel. Ever since she got wind of the rock, she felt her luck was changing. Her life had been a series of disappointments, from not being born pretty to not being the favorite child to not being wed to not being a mother to not being a grandmother. Not that it mattered, because she didn't even like kids. Not that she discriminated; she didn't like anyone. She especially didn't like foreigners. And most of all, she didn't like her neighbors!

The woman called herself Missus Drager so nobody would know that she was an old maid. That she hadn't been chosen. For anything. Other kids didn't like her as a child. Co-workers never liked her. She once bought a pet on a lonesome whim. The cat scratched and bit her then scrammed.

This was a chance to finally have something. And maybe the money would buy her respect. It might even make her be liked.

Otherwise, she might just lose it someday and go off on one of those rampages she would hear about in the news. It was desperate people like her, frayed around the edges, feeling left out and unloved.

Minerva forded across the intersection. A bicycle for two with a length of spring in the middle, the rear section boinging, whizzed by.

A chassis minus the car chugged before her, driven by a test-dummy.

A man wearing suspenders and a derby pedalled past, holding an open umbrella on an old-fashioned two-wheeler with an oversize front tire.

Spiro and Driscoll scurried after, almost getting plowed into by a team of horses carting a yesteryear fire-engine. Beyond the juncture, the trio came to a railroad depot. Minerva brashly entered the station, hoping to find the girl. The passengers waiting for their train must have been sitting there for decades. The men, women, and children were dressed in outmoded attire. Their forms were translucent, faded. They were specters haunting the depot, yet the three living individuals did not so much as acknowledge the fact, for not one of them believed in ghosts.

It's one of those topics that people either accept or don't, like aliens. A steadfast principle to most, as hard-line and unyielding as religion or politics. A flying saucer could land on the head of a scoffer like Minerva and she would claim it never happened. Thus, the revenants made no impression. They were greeted as ordinary persons, which is to say that they were not greeted at all.

Missus Drager interrogated the skeleton dressed as a stationmaster behind the Ticket Window. "Have you seen a girl in a black jacket? I think she has a bag. It might be blue."

"Nope. Ain't seen nobody like that," the boneman whispered. He couldn't speak very well without lungs.

A bell began to toll. A whistle shrieked. Rumbling arose. A locomotive clattered to the station then halted, metal frictioning.

Those waiting on benches filed to the platform. Clouds of steam obscured the train. Minerva, Spiro, and Driscoll watched as a single passenger disembarked. The ghosts climbed aboard and the train rolled out of the station.

An incredibly tall thin man bent his neck, ducking into the depot. He wore a gray vest and coat, snug striped trousers, black boots. In his hand he carried a gray wide-brimmed hat with a curved crown.

"Evening, madam," he stated to Missus Drager. "Allow me to announce myself: I am Mister Thaddeus. They call me The Gray Man. I am the one who patrols the regions between. Right and Wrong. Left and Right. In and Out. Above, Below." He aimed an index finger up and down to illustrate.

"Have you seen a girl?" was all Minerva wanted to know.

Mister Thaddeus ahemmed. His nose was of a distinctive quality in that it jutted rather far. His face was oval, his eyebrows dark and well-defined. Irises were gray. He had a trim mouth and sharp chin. There were many girls, he responded, and he had seen a fair amount of them. "Exactly the one you mean could be any one of those. Or any one who is not one of the particular ones I have seen."

He leaned toward Minerva, his neck straightening, nose to nose. "Why do you inquire? Is there a purpose? Have you an issue to resolve? Perhaps a gray-area matter to be settled? I am quite adept with such intricacies. Ask anyone!" He waved a hand, although the station was deserted but for them. Even the skeleton had departed (or had fallen to the floor of the ticket office).

Missus Drager hemmed and hawed. She couldn't tell him why, that she wanted to steal a gem. Or how: by any means possible — for she was ruthless when it came to her desires, and defending her entitlements. She couldn't tell him who because she didn't know the girl's identity, had never striven to pay attention.

"It's nothing, really. I'm simply trying to return something that I borrowed," she lied.

The Gray Man

It was a preposterous falsity. But it wasn't as if this fellow hadn't heard every deception and ruse and excuse, every twist and tangle and untruth. To recognize the gray, he had to see the good and bad, the furthest extremes. It went with the territory.

The Gray Man hmmed, or perhaps he hummed. "I can see that you are acquainted with the peripheries of grayness. I shall pass your message on if I should meet her and it seems pertinent. But if I met her and something else should fit, then I would tell her that instead." He uttered a significant admonition: "Watch your footing in the shadows. It can get a good bit slippery!"

Mister Thaddeus pivoted to exit the station. He stood vertical then tamped his hat upon his head. The man produced a notebook and pen from his coat, etched a few jots. Snapping it shut, he tucked the pad away and pulled an ornate pewter walking stick from his sleeve. He strutted off with his posture tipped back, smacking the bottom of the staff on the platform.

"Well, he's a twit and this was a waste of time!" crabbed Missus Drager. She barged out the door to churn the opposite direction.

Driscoll and Spiro followed, each vying to stay behind the other — one not wishing to turn his back; the second maliciously wanting to give due cause for concern.

21

A SIGN INFORMED ME the distance was nine miles to my destination. I was numb by then from cold and aches and all-out misery. Gimping along, I didn't know if I had it in me to make it that far — if I ever had it, let alone if I had any of it left. What I did know was that I was absolutely determined not to go back into the trees!

But this was before I met the old lady. She, too, plodded beside the highway. Oddly, I hadn't noticed her, like she was suddenly there in front of me. I should have figured it was pretty strange and been wary. You'd think I would have learned something after all I had been through.

She was just an elderly woman clad in a shawl. She could have been somebody's grandma. Could have if she had been human.

Maybe she *was* in a technical sense. I don't wish to imply that all witches are bad. Everyone has civil rights these days; even, I suppose, witches and warlocks. But there had been nothing ordinary or common about her despite a benign appearance. Instead of baking cookies for grandchildren, she was likelier baking children in her oven. I wouldn't put anything past somebody who carried dead toads in her purse. I saw them when she opened it quickly to offer me a stick of gum. Thinking of Rhonda, consoled by the association, I accepted — although my motto with strangers, and in uncomfortable or unfamiliar situations, was to simply say no. Even upon receiving it to be polite, I shouldn't have unwrapped and placed the tainted token in my mouth.

Also, she seemed to not be in a hurry to get somewhere when I observed her up ahead. It was as if she were larcenously dawdling on purpose so I would catch up.

I was delighted to glimpse a fellow pedestrian, laggard or not. One who didn't look like he or she or it was from another solar system, another dimension; who didn't consist of sulfur and bile. One who was more normal than I was. Still, there was something about this woman that didn't add up. She was weird, but I couldn't quite place what I didn't like or trust or comprehend about her. It wasn't obvious.

As for the part about being a witch, that was even less conspicuous. But I should have guessed. I have a nose for trouble, let us not forget. It was awfully dense of me to be so thick. Maybe I had an excuse. Maybe all of the above and being scared witless should cut me some slack.

Sure, there was no hairy wart on her nose or chin. Her complexion wasn't green, and she wasn't wearing a pointy hat or riding a broom. Reality witches are not the Halloween clichés we give them credit for. So how was I supposed to tell? It might have been her ripe odor, or the cobwebs in her hair. It might have been the wisp of black fabric peeping out from under the normal old-lady attire, or the trollish barbarity slurking just behind a sugarcoated smile. Those little clues so offbeat or innocuous that we can convince ourselves they are of no consequence.

When I jogged to overtake her, the woman acted as if she did not expect to see me. "Oh, my! You gave me such a fright. Where are you going, dear?" That smile dripped with honey, masking the stings of a killer-bee swarm.

I told her I was lost, headed for the next town.

"But that's miles away!" Her grandmotherly veneer, the flower-pattern gingham dress and silver hair-bun, the sensible shoes and swollen pantyhosed ankles were patently disarming. "I live much closer. Why don't you come there? I'll make us a pot of tea. This dark road isn't safe for a pretty girl like you!"

"I need to phone my aunt," I vocalized. "And there are some bodies to report to the police."

"You're welcome to use my telephone. Please say yes!" the woman blandished. And gave me a piece of gum. "I'd enjoy the company. And you must be hungry. I know I am. I could bake a nice casserole, or cook a steaming kettle of soup!"

"That would be lovely," I assented. My stomach was audibly panging. I believed my luck was improving.

"It is lovely." Her grin was smug. "Here's my lane."

We angled off the highway onto a muddy trail with a partition of plants. I pegged my foreboding to the ominous rustle of trees as we strolled side by side in parallel tracks. Shoulder to shoulder, we were about the same shortness.

"Adeline Gruelsby," the woman introduced. "Call me Addy. What's your name, dear?"

"Arletta Trimble."

We came to a stone cottage. She pushed the door, which was unlocked, and we were bathed by a reddish glow from a lamp with a ruby glass shade.

In the light Adeline looked ninety or older, yet a robust ninety. Wrinkles upon wrinkles fanned out from her features. There was a spiderish raptitude about her eyes. "You remind me of myself at your age," she commented.

I nodded. What could I say? It might be a compliment, or it could be an insult. I didn't know which since I didn't know much about her, including the part about being a witch.

Addy closed the door firmly, murmuring below
her breath. I would later discover it was a binding spell
to seal the portal and keep me from escaping.

Walls were lined with shelves containing every size,
color, shape of jar and bottle. These were full of powders
and spices and other ingredients.

A huge iron crucible frothed over the fire in an
enormous hearth. My immediate thought: How could
one old lady eat so much soup? She was rather obese
but still . . . Did she bring strangers home every day
to feed? Was this like a soup kitchen for charity?

The cauldron gave me the first proof that witchery
was afoot. I just didn't realize it then.

Adeline had a very large oven for one person as well.
Big enough to fit an entire person within. Not that such
a notion entered my conscious mind at that moment.
My nervous nose was acting up. My intellect was
impervious.

The woman had but one meager table and a single
chair. Upon it sat a solitary bowl and spoon; a singular
goblet. These were all contradictions! But do you think
a bell rang in my brain? Do you think I put two and two
together and derived that three is *not* the correct sum?

I certainly didn't. I am a dunderhead when it
comes to Arithmetic.

What *did* bong a chord and spark the dawn of
comprehension was the fact that Adeline had no phone.
As I gazed around, that discrepancy sank in like a boulder.
Heart in my esophagus, I quit ignoring my nose and began
to heed more daunting portents. There were quite a few!

Some of the jars had shocking labels . . .
Crossed-Eye Of Newborn.
Big Toe Of Little Girl.
Left Ear Of Priest.
Virtue Of Virgin.
Lips Of Liar.
Bite Of Vampire.

Hair Of Werewolf.
Zombie Brains.
Nose Of Puppet.
Mitten Of Bat.
Head Of Lettuce.
Foot In Mouth.
Broken Leg Of Actor.
Room Of Elbow.
Thumb Of Hitcher.
Knee Of Kneeler.
Squat Of Squatter.

There were quantities of Lady Fingers, Baby Teeth, Cherub Cheeks, Lost Youth.

And Double Chins, Locked Jaws, Tied Tongues, Hanged Nails.

Mince and meat pies must have been filled with ground-up children, for a pint-sized finger obtruded from a crust. Brownies had teeth for nuts. Mondo cupcakes had still-beating hearts.

A black feline purred in a corner. And if that weren't enough, the closet held a broomstick and pointy hat. Panic throttled me. I couldn't make a sound. The witch yanked off her wig and frock to reveal an unwashed white mane, a black dress. The transformation was hideous.

"You'll make a tender morsel, my dear!" relished the crone. "A bit skimpy, but you'll do for a snack. Shall I bake you or boil you? And what parts should I keep? I know! You have a secret, don't you? I collect secrets!"

She flounced to a small dark bottle with a cork. Lifting the vial she exulted, "You can't keep a secret from me, girl. So out with it or I'll have to pry it from you! First your tongue and then your brain!" The hag cackled with boisterous zeal.

"My middle name is Tallulah," I blurted. A hand flew to my mouth.

The Witch

Adeline chittered. "It's that gum I gave you. Before putting you to sleep, it will make you confess your deepest thoughts!"

"Often I've wondered what fish think of us when they look through the glass," my tongue tattled.

"That isn't deep!" screeched the witch. "Concentrate! There is something you know. Something that's hidden."

"I've always wanted to be a window washer. I like their doohickey that goes up and down. And they see a lot of fascinating people on the other side of the panes."

I had no idea where this was coming from. Perhaps it was related to the fish thing.

"Deeper! You must go deeper!" Adeline shrilled.

"I think friends are like Lucky Pennies. When you find one you should always keep it, because you can use all the luck you can get. And one day, if you've found enough, you will find yourself rich!" my mouth blabbed. I sounded like a greeting card, or a fortune cookie.

"Keep going!"

"Sometimes I ask myself, why does a rotten apple have to spoil the whole barrel? Why can't the good apples mend the bad one? Of course if it's beyond repair, wormy and putrid and festering, I suppose then they would have to get rid of it."

"All the way down! To the underbelly of your lowest intestine!" screamed the witch.

"My aunt is up to something. I think she's in cahoots with the doctor," I unburdened. Wow, neither my nose nor my intuition had seen that coming either! "And I really don't like gum," I cynically corollaried, spitting it out at her face. The wad adhered to her nose.

About then it occurred to me that I had an ace up my sleeve.

In my sack, more accurately. I didn't know what might turn up there, but it had saved me before. I had to hope it would come through again.

I remembered dumping everything out with the salt. What if I poured out the magic too? What if it was just an empty bag?

The witch muttered an incantation. I couldn't hear what she was saying but it didn't sound good. She wanted my secret. What secret? The only secret I had was a secret weapon, and maybe I didn't even have that anymore!

Reaching into the flat messenger bag, I fished around but nothing magically presented itself in my palm. Fretfully I resorted to Plan B and made a dash for the door. The biddy had blocked it with a spell.

There was no latch, yet try as I might it wouldn't budge. I stuck my hand in the sack as the witch advanced, mumbling magic phrases and waggling the spike-nailed digits of the hand without the blue bottle as if to tickle me. I doubted that was her intent. She wanted to catch me and shove me into her oven, or the bubbling cauldron.

My fingers gripped a cold metal handle!

I extracted a mirror and jubilantly flouted it at the hag's face. I couldn't cudgel her with it, for the glass would have shattered and brought me bad luck. I held it up so she could view herself, and that did the trick.

Adeline squawped, her head shaking in abominy, eyes bugging. There were no mirrors in her home because the sight of her own true ugliness was so unbearable to an evil witch that scrutinizing her countenance would blind her. Vanity was the bruha's utmost conceit. She could render herself beautiful through enchantments, but in her house the truth came out.

This harpy's orbs exploded, spurting blood at the mirror. She howled and clawed at me, her talons long and curved. I pressed the mirror into her clasp. She venomously hurled it to a wall. Glass splintered, showering the floor. The bad luck was on *her*.

Face gory, the witch stumbled after my footsteps. I was trapped and could only run in circles. My head was woozy, the sleeping spell taking effect. Passing shelves, I threw jars and bottles at my pursuer. The harridan snarled savagely, too distracted to cast a spell.

Thinking herself clever, she feinted and lunged at me. Groggily I dodged, evading her clutches, and she was propelled by her momentum straight into the boiling crucible of broth.

Yawning, I found myself oddly curious — even as the woman's legs kicked their last and submerged — if she ate from the cauldron in which she brewed her potions. It was too late to ask.

With the witch's demise, the door of her cottage swung open. Broken, too, was the spell on the gum. I retreated to the highway through a wrathful storm of wind and forest debris . . . more determined than ever *not* to repeat the colossal error of entering the woods.

22

CAMILLE AND NIGEL hastened through the shifting turns and twists of their labyrinthine environment, anxious to locate the same illusive young lady the rest of them were looking for, who seemed to be gone with the wind. Of course, this wasn't an easy thing to tell since the cloudscape was hardly finite. It went on and on in an endless dreamland of layers and levels. They couldn't find an exit, let alone one measly girl.

The bickersome couple, who exemplified an uncomfortable-shoe relationship based on attraction and convenience more than compatibility and affection, irascibly stumped forth into the storm. And the storm was indeed stormy, splashing them in precipitous waves by the bucket, regaling them with blasts of windred guff. Waterlogged, heads down, they quavered through. Until the bowling-ball-sized hail percussing about them caused them to scramble in trepidation. They emerged from the inclemence panting and soaked, taking shelter in a chamber.

The vault's contents amounted to a single carton. More of a crate. Stamped in red on the front were the words DO NOT OPEN.

"What do you think is in there?" Camille speculated.

"Nothing good," pronounced her beau, adjusting his glasses above his nose after attempting to dry them with a soggy handkerchief.

"But how do we know unless we open it?"

"We know because it says not to open it," the doctor pragmatically construed. "And because there has not been a single good thing in this place since we arrived!"

"I suppose you're right." Camille's tone was reluctant. "But what if you're wrong? What if there's something valuable? Or a pile of money?"

Greed was one of the Seven Sins. It was also one of their common traits.

Nigel's interest was piqued so he acquiesced that one little peek wouldn't hurt. Applying manual labor and elbow grease, with a fair deal of sputtering, he loosened a corner of the wood box. Boosting the edge, his eyes strained to see within. Everything was blurry through his smeared lenses. Raising them, he squinted at the box's interior.

"What is it?" Camille avidly grilled.

"I can't tell, it's too dark. Help me with this." Together they levered the lid higher and dislodged a second corner. As they pushed the cover off, a jinn uncoiled — swaying, buoyant, grinning.

The genie embodied an airy demeanor and a puggish impertinent visage. "You lose!" was his pompous decree. "You looked inside!"

Camille scorned, "Of course we did, what else could we do? It begged to be opened. It was a puzzle box!"

"A box does not need to be opened when it is intended to be closed," indicted the windsprite.

"Well, that's a fine thanks after letting you out," sulked Camille.

"You didn't let me out, I let you in!" The genie folded his arms. He had no legs, just a funneling tail that stemmed from the box.

Nigel blinked at the jinn from beneath his eyeglasses. "Aren't you supposed to grant us wishes or something?"

"I will grant one wish," the genie indulged. "Before you are punished for your crimes! Choose wisely, for it will be your last request."

The part about punishment failed to register. Nigel and Camille excitedly conferred over what to ask for. Camille wanted a mansion full of money. Nigel wanted a yacht full of gold. They couldn't compromise.

Out of patience, the jinn decided for them: "You shall live."

The two humans felt gypped. "We're already alive!" they chorused.

"Then you should be grateful. I am allowing you to stay alive. For now," spoke the genie. "Be gone!" He clapped and hurtled them from the chamber.

Anzillu refolded his arms and, with a genie bob of the head, vanished into himself.

23

IT WAS STILL an imposing distance to Woebegone.
I wasn't confident my legs would hold out. Fatigue made
me feel like vomiting. It was causing my anxiety to swell,
my mind to think of gloom and despair. My emotions
were stretched thin. And I had blisters on top of blisters
by now. If I paused to rest, my leg muscles would cramp.

Walking off a charley-horse, I was astonished
to hear a motor vehicle. Could it be that easy???
Was salvation going to come to me instead of my having
to hike thirteen miles through a maelstrom of wind and
rain and peculiarities? I should have known that it was
too good to be true, but being an optimist most of the
time left me like a beggar with my hand out for trouble.

Didn't my nose alert me? you might ask. I think
it was too cold. I wasn't dressed very warm, so all of me
was chilled. I trembled from a triple-whammy of weather,
fear, and nerves.

Headlamps shone. A shiny black sedan pulled
alongside me. The driver lowered his window. "Evening,
miss! You look like you could use a lift," he greeted in
an amiable voice. He drove a large car but he was kind
of puny and his eyes were wobbly. Other than that,
he seemed okay.

All of the warnings against hitching a ride don't
take into account that you might be stranded in the
wilderness, desperate for help. I had no option but
to accept.

It's not like he had a sign on his forehead saying AXE MURDERER. If he did, sore and frozen and overwrought as I was, I might have still decided to take my chances. But since he didn't have a sign, it was one of those things where it had been decided before it was even asked.

Hopping in on the passenger side, smiling at the driver, I informed him my name was Arletta Trimble and I needed to go to Woebegone. Or the nearest phone. If he had a phone I could borrow, that would be better, yet I still needed to go somewhere. I didn't care to be abandoned on the roadside.

The man didn't have a telephone. He did have some unusual mannerisms. When he spoke his eyeballs wiggled. When he smiled his eyes crossed. When he frowned, well, he just frowned — his eyebrows scrunched together. If he laughed, his eyes rolled in every direction. I found this rather strange. It seemed perfectly harmless, however, so I wasn't too alarmed.

Another eccentric thing he did was that he listened to static on the radio. That's right, static! If music began to hone in on his fizzing and popping, he would fiddle with the dial until it was nothing but pure unadulterated white noise again.

An irrelevant quirk was his outfit. He had on a beige trenchcoat completely buttoned up to his neck. It looked funny, that's all.

Glancing at the rear seat, I noticed stacks upon stacks of black books. They looked like Bibles. "Are you a Bible salesman?" I queried, just to make conversation. I was really bad at conversation, but even I could think of asking something obvious.

"No." He seemed uncomfortable.

"You don't have to be embarrassed. It's an honorable profession," I soothed. "Although it's more of a career than a profession."

He literally squirmed in his seat. "I don't sell Bibles." In other words, drop the subject.

Being analytical, I couldn't drop a subject until it was ready to be dropped. As in, until there was no question about it. No ifs, ands, or buts too.

"Then what kind of books *do* you sell?" I quizzed.

His temper went out the window. Possibly because he forgot to wind it up. "I don't sell books!" he fumed.

"Then why is your backseat full of them?" I wondered.

"They're not mine!" His conviviality had been replaced by a sourpuss expression.

"Whose are they?"

"Somebody else's!" When he was angry, the man's eyes turned rosy.

I could see I was getting nowhere so I mentioned, "By the way, you never told me your name."

"Stop interrogating me!" the guy exhorted. And slammed the brakes.

We had only driven about a mile. The next marker for Woebegone was visible. The driver commanded, "Get out."

I was stupefied, my jaw hanging.

"Go on, get out," he reiterated.

"You can't kick me out when you're rescuing me!" I protested.

"Yes I can if you ask too many questions!" he insisted.

"What if I refuse?" I was curious how he was going to make me.

This made him madder than a cow. "You can't. It's my car!"

"Prove it. Show me the registration," I demanded.

Which made him madder than a hatter. The guy unlatched his door and clumbered from the vehicle. I heard his shoes clop to the trunk. A key scraped. The hatch sprang up with a squeal of hinges.

He fished inside. I heard some weird sounds.
That got me curiouser. I opened my door, stepped out,
tippy-toed to the end of the car and gasped.

A dead man in a tweed suit was crammed into the
trunk. Whoa! The man with the crazed eyes was a killer!
This must be the Bible salesman, I connected. Also the
owner of the car.

The maniac rummaged.

I know what you're thinking: He pulled out an
axe. *Ehhhh!* Wrong answer. He turned into an evil elf
with pointed ears and pikish teeth. *Then* he pulled out
an axe.

Luridly gleering, Elvish hefted the massive
Viking-size chopper.

Oh boy. Blowing on my right hand for luck,
I reached into my bag. And hoped that I wouldn't
draw a smaller axe. I didn't. It was a bigger one.

Wielding my weapon with difficulty, I didn't
cherish being roped into an axe battle. Fortunately
for me, the elf spotted my kingly hacker and dropped
his. I won by default.

Leaping behind the steering wheel, he sped off
peeling rubber.

I was left standing by the wayside. Perhaps
it would be best to walk, I conceded. And so I did.

The Axe-Murderous Elf

24

TONKA HESITANTLY JUMPED through a flaming hoop. It wasn't the usual hoop employed in circus acts for tigers and such. It was a portal. Rhonda came next, then Terence and Juniper. They found themselves in a sunny sector of the storm inhabited by floating womb globs with sleeping babies, animated toys, nursery-rhymish animals, and fanciful cloud shapes.

"This place is so happy!" cheered Rhonda. "Let's stay here awhile!"

"We cannot," Tonka reprimanded. "Meezly needs us. She could be in jeopardy! You must not be led astray!"

"Dis is an evil place. We must remember dat," cautioned Juniper.

"Es muy oscuro," remarked Terence as the wayfarers throve to a shadowed region at the back of the sunshine, where waspy figures slithed and slunkered in quarrelous paroxysms of shadiness. The eventudes strove to enshroud them by casting nets of deceitful blemished subterfuge. Tonka led them past the quagmire, slashing his baton to keep the darkness at bay.

They needed to find their friend. This storm was trying to obstruct and detain them. The group halted before a steep gorge. The path began crumbling behind them. Tonka aimed his wand. There was no leeway, no margin for mistakes.

"We must prevail. Expand the trail," he chanted.

A tightrope extended across the void into a bank of fog. What lay beyond was a mystery. "Everyone form a chain!" Tonka bade.

Juniper hugged his waist. Ronnie hugged Juniper and Terence hugged Rhonda. They stepped onto the wire. "You must believe you can do it," instructed Tonka. The four moved as one, inching their feet, moving like a caterpillar on a blade of grass.

Near the center of the distance, the wind started in. Then sheets of moisture. The rope became slippery. "Hang on!" yelled Tonka over the furor. Obeying his own advice, clinching his hat brim, he thrust the rod to oppose the air and waterworks. Magical forces clashed in a cacophony of sound, an opulence of light.

The atmosphere rippled. The storm was squelched. But the four clinging friends were knocked from the wire.

25

MY INTRINSIC JOURNEY of the soul began and would end with the stone I was enlisted to find, entrusted to safeguard. It seemed to have nothing to do with my present circumstances, and I seemed to have no hope of encountering it while trapped on Highway Zero. That worried me, for I take commitments to heart and needed to carry out my father's request. At any cost.

We sometimes get wrapped up in something that isn't worth a life, isn't worth placing it all on the line, but we give it all we've got and endanger health or sanity towards achieving a goal we think vitally important at the time. Just as we may get disproportionately upset over some trivial thing and risk harming ourselves or another by reckless deeds.

This wasn't like that. My mission, I believed, was one of those glorious noble undertakings you read about in storybook legends. I wasn't exaggerating or risking my friends and myself over nothing. Whatever I had to go through would be necessary to lead me to that destiny I had been bequeathed.

If you are given a loftier purpose, or a reason in your life to praise the heavens and the stars, you cease to worry about past regrets once you've realized the key: Had anything major (possibly minor) not gone precisely as it did, everything could change. It might be better or it might be worse. It might just be completely different. But it wouldn't be the way it is or was. It would be something else entirely.

And if you treasure what you have or had along the way, then regrets are like dead skin. We need to let them go, let them slough off and waft away or subside to the ground as we venture on.

Happiness is like that. It is a choice. It can be transitory, a case of perspective, a windfall we didn't foresee. But if we embrace its positive restorative marvels, it will transform us into something greater than we were before. And if we focus on that, the unhappy things tend to relinquish their control of us. They shrink in comparison, and we are left better for it.

Therefore, I couldn't refuse to travel this road. I couldn't stand still, or wake up yet. I was meant to be here and so I had to keep going, had to move forward. That was all I knew. This wasn't random, and my steps along the turnpike had to take me where I needed to go, get me where I needed to be to find that stone.

Whatever must be sacrificed in terms of time and energy, the comforts of home, that was what I had to do.

I didn't know then how very much it mattered to follow that road.

My feet exceeded the point of pain. I was colder than a naked polar bear as I staggered down an asphalt ribbon between hostile pines. I had to rouse the strength from deep inside, tapping a reservoir of willpower . . . I wasn't used to so much exertion. Amazing what we can endure when we have to. When pumped on adrenaline and there seems no alternative.

Headlights twinkled ahead. I braced for trouble. My nose was out of commission, being an icicle, but my intuition was signalling to flee the highway. Where was I going to run, if I could run — back to the trees? I felt safer on the road. I moved over to the shoulder and hoped for the best. The way my day was going, I wasn't expecting much.

Two motorcycles came whining around a bend. I clamped my ears, the engines were so loud. They braked abruptly on the blacktop, which glistened from a recent drizzle. Spray arose and the bikes angled skidding, smashing, sparking and scraping pavement.

A pair of riders crawled out of the wreckage then turned to trudge diagonally across the lanes. Both wore all black: denim jeans and jackets; glossy dark helmets, the visors tinted. I halted since they were beelining straight towards me. A few feet away they stopped too, removed and discarded their headgear. I thought I was prepared for anything. I wasn't.

They had no faces. Least, that was my assumption. Thick blond hair hung down, tucked into the zippered collars of their jackets, no bumps for noses or chins.

"What do we have here?" asked one with a breathy high-pitched voice.

Was that a rhetorical question? I wondered. Or was I supposed to respond?

Before I could come up with a reply, the other gave a henchman chortle then said in a lower-pitched breathy voice, "It appears to be a girl."

"That it does," nodded the first. His cranium swiveled. There was a face after all, and I wished there wasn't. He was shockingly deformed with mismatched eyes, from large and bulging to beady. A meaty honker that drooped and was lopsided. A cleft upper lip with teeth exposed. And a sagging puffy throat under a weak chin.

His biker bud's noodle rotated, and this guy was even more misshapen. His nose and eyes were tiny, and his mouth was huge with bloated lips. A plump tongue crept out at intervals. He had boils and red splotches and furrows. His eyebrows were like bushy mustaches, and he had some long hairs, not many, dangling from nostrils and chin. A stream of slobber dribbled.

"She looks tasty, don't you think?" commended his brother.

"I *am* kind of famished," claimed his sibling.

"We missed lunch."

"That we did."

"Shall we eat her raw?"

"It would be faster."

"You can have the first bite," offered Big Nose.

"You're too kind," vaunted Big Mouth.

By then I had picked up on the fact that they planned to make me dinner, as the main course, like the witch and the vampire, the tree and the root man. The lake monster had artistic designs. The elf — I still wasn't sure what he had in mind. I was just glad I didn't find out.

It was time for the bag to do its magic. Before I could reach in, Big Mouth grabbed my right arm. Big Nose seized the left.

My heart was thudding like a washer with an uneven load.

The brothers started dickering.

"I get the legs."

"No, we'll share. We each get a leg and an arm."

"Okay, I want the eyes!"

"There are two. We'll split them. There's only one nose. You can have that. But I get the tongue!"

"I want the tongue! You take the nose!"

"You had the tongue last night."

"It was bitter! This one looks sweet."

"You can't always have the sweet tongues!" hashed Big Nose.

"I know how to settle this," I interfered.

"How?" they asked.

"You could draw straws. I have some in my bag. I'll show you."

"This tongue is smart too," hungered Big Mouth.

The Biker Brothers

They courteously unhanded me. My fingers delved inside the sack, but it was empty! I had been overconfident, daring to believe, expecting a miracle, only to come up with a palmful of air!

"Well?" they demanded.

I groped in my bag again. "They have to be here somewhere," I muttered. I wasn't really after straws, yet I figuratively seemed to be grasping at them.

"She's stalling!" contempted Big Mouth.

"That she is! And with our tongue!" Big Nose affricted.

They resumed their food fight, which turned into a bloody spat. The mutant cannibal twins released me to engage in fisticuffs. With any luck, it would turn into a deadly brawl.

Unfortunately it didn't. Their bellies growled like a supper bell, and the feud was postponed for a bite to eat. Stifling an impulse to wet myself, I quailishly tried the bag once more. My clammy fingers discovered a firmly soft and imperfectly round object: a purple plum.

I polished the plum on my jacket, praying the mutant sibs liked fruit as much as flesh. "Oh, how tantalizing," I crooned. "I bet it's sweeter than my tongue. What a pity, there's only one!"

Drooling, the brothers went back to scuffling. The plum was so tender and juicy a prize that they fracassed to the finish.

I dropped the plum on their torn and lifeless bodies then continued down the road, passing pieces of the motorcycles. The bikes were totalled, not that I knew how to operate one anyway or cared to either. Life was perilous enough without increasing the risks. I didn't even drive a car. I was too nervous. Most of the time I'd rather walk. I just wished my feet weren't ready to fall off.

26

GOURD WAS AWAKENING INSIDE, aware that he had a heart however badly scarred. He had not been so turbulent within for a very long while. He felt alive. Existing in a taciturn dolorous state was not a life. Just as feeling something, anything, was better than feeling no pain — even if it kept the demons submerged.

He had gone through each day in abject melancholy, when he permitted emotion, or a state of nothingness when he did not. But now he was reviving, coming out of hibernation, because his instincts told him that there was something to care about again . . .

Killing his friend had been the hardest thing he ever did as a soldier.

The second time he killed him as a cop. His mind replayed the scene when he was called on the phone by a voice from the grave. Mason summoned him to the site of a hostage crisis at a public location, a gymnasium. He had a bag filled with guns and ammunition. He had fifteen captives, women and men, from trainers to fitness clients. He was rigged with explosives. What Gourd didn't know was that the hostages were also wired to blow.

Mason demanded that Gourd enter the gym unarmed.

Richard eased through the doors, walked slowly toward his resurrected pal, hands to the sides. "Let's talk about this," he said.

"The time to talk was before you pulled the trigger."
Mason patted him, searching for a weapon, then shoved
him to a bench. They were in the Weight Room. Hostages
stood against a wall, blindfolded with cloth wrappings or
martial-arts belts, as if for a firing squad. "Now it's the
time for action!" asserted the gunman. Dressed in
camouflage jacket and trousers, military boots,
he bared the explosives strapped to his abdomen
and chest.

He resembled the stereotypic mass murderer on
a rampage. He was, in fact, a cold-blooded systematic
serial killer with a string of homicides to his "credit",
the man bragged. He had moved around, used a variety
of methods. He had been thinning the herd for many
years without being caught. He was ready to be stopped
but he wanted to go out in style. And he wanted to take
the man who betrayed him along.

Not every war vet became a mass murderer,
the kind who made the news. But most had to live
with a degree of guilt from the blood on their hands
of their fellow man, whether innocent or not. Being
shipped off to combat, pushed into a kill-or-be-killed
situation, logic dictates to fight or retreat. In the
objectivity born of time, war ethics and the passion
of gung-ho call-of-duty patriotism could fade. Gourd
bowed his head. He was responsible for his own
transgressions, and for the torment of these people.
For all of the victims over the years since the bullets
he fired neglected to end this man's spree of violence.

"You get it now, don't you?" laughed Mason.
"That it's your fault. You let me go. You let me
get away."

Richard wasn't sure whether his war buddy felt
betrayed for being shot, or for not being killed.

"You wanted me to," Gourd flatly stated. "But
it wasn't my intention."

"You're not going to get out of this, old friend. We're not going to salvage each other this time." Mason directed the muzzle of an automatic rifle toward the line-up of captives.

Gourd reacted by lunging, but Mason spun to slam him in the head with the butt of the rifle. Richard was propelled backwards, knocking the bench over and collapsing behind it. A detonation left him temporarily deaf.

Forehead bloody, Gourd sat up in horror to find the room demolished. He would blame himself for the explosion.

The scar on his brow throbbed, as if triggered by the memory. Like a homing device, he turned according to the sharpest pains down a series of tunnels until arriving at an impasse. The end of the maze. A plain door-shaped brick wall. It wasn't just a dead-end. This was where he needed to go.

The detective pressed the bricks, searching for loose mortar. Locating the lever, he pulled and a panel swung wide. The agony of his scar acute, Gourd stepped through the gate.

27

IT HAD BEEN STORMING on and off. My clothes were
damp, which made them colder and more uncomfortable.
My teeth chattered as I trudged stiff and sore down the
turnpike. I practically didn't care what happened next.
I just wanted to get it over with. Every mile there was
some new atrocity. A pattern had been repeating like
a motif, and I was the central character that linked
these raving-mad elements.

Well, whatever came next, I hoped it wouldn't
defeat me. Somehow I was surviving all this. Me —
the runty introvert who didn't make friends easily until
the previous year when I found myself in the midst of
a pretty awesome posse.

They had found me, to be truthful, because
I wasn't very outgoing. Even prior to losing my family.
I don't know why. I think I had always been waiting
for the right moment. Some people waited too long.
The moment passed and they couldn't find it again.
Like trying to fall asleep. I had friends through the
years, but not the kind who stayed with you and
wouldn't dream of letting you drift away. I never
had that.

Even my parents were gone.

Aunt Camille and I weren't actually that close,
so she didn't count. I scarcely knew her. She was
Dad's sister, and she had never shown any real interest
in me. She came into the picture *after* my parents were
out of it. I figured she felt sorry for me, and decided
to be the aunt she hadn't bothered to be in the past.

She couldn't take the place of my parents. Nobody could. I had lost them too soon. I thought there would be more time. For a year I mourned, then Dad's letter gave me a chance to ascend from that rut. It gave me a reason to move forward.

The previous year had been the lowest point in my life. And yet, when I was at my least confident, I had finally formed some lasting friendships. The kind I didn't have to worry about accepting me; they simply did. But it wasn't fair. Why must I sacrifice one good thing to gain another?

Moodily I plodded, feeling sorry for myself, unable to shirk the weight of the maudlin self-pity that had joined me on this lonesome trek.

A large puddle loomed along the side of the pavement. There must have been a moon. Light gilded the surface. I loitered, staring down, viewing my reflection. My hair was wild and tangled from wind and precipitation. My beret flattened, absorbing the rain. My face so blank and timid. Was this who I had become? When had I changed? My friends didn't see this frightened image. I was different with them than I was alone. Different with my parents too. Was it that they didn't know the real me? Or that I didn't know this person who looked so scared?

It was tough to balance how I saw myself, how I felt inside, and how others saw me. My equilibrium had tipped *before* an ill wind gusted through my life. It wasn't this one night. It had started long ago.

The puddle blooped, which *really* threw me off balance!

The mirror smoothed. I saw myself as a little girl. Then Aunt Camille was there, snapping at me to hurry. I was crying.

She was supposed to watch me on a stormy black-and-white evening. Instead she tried to sell me, first to gypsies — who told her that the meme about them stealing and buying children was a myth — and then to an adoption ring. Camille was angry that my father wouldn't invest in horseradishes, one of her many enterprising schemes. I had been kept in a trailer with other stolen kids. The police busted the ring that night and rescued us. My aunt promised to stay away if my parents wouldn't press charges. Too late, my aplomb had been dimmed. At heart I was an optimist with an effervescent character, but my innate bubbliness had undergone some bursting.

I heard a voice from within the shallow pool. A fey crackly timbre, exuding a netherworldly surfeit of grief. I couldn't decipher what it was saying and had to lean nearer. "Are you talking to me?"

"That depends. Who are you?" sighed the mud-puddle.

"Arletta Trimble," I informed it. "And who might you be?"

"Duh. Anyone can see that I'm a puddle."

"Yes, but you're not always a puddle. What are you when there's no rain?"

I *had* to ask these questions! The puddle reared up into a golemesque monster to show me.

I leaped backwards, ogling the beast. He splooshed onto the highway in pursuit. How did I get myself into these messes? I pondered. And this was messier than most, I had to admit. I was no fan of mud baths or smearing mud on my face to look younger. Maybe when I was older I would sing a different tune, but at present mud held no appeal whatsoever.

The mudman invected, "I am not to be trifled with! You will give me what I seek!"

"All right, if you insist."

As he sploshed towards me, I did what I was accustomed to doing in these dilemmas. I stuck my hand in the sack, curious to see what might bail me out of this. The bag always knew. I had no idea.

My hand wrapped around a handle.

I withdrew a racket to my surprise. "Tennis, anyone?" I lampoonishly jested.

The beast did not appreciate my droll wit or backhanded humor. Nor did he care for my forehand as I swung the racket through his soft composition, serving bits of him onto the road. He was no "match" for me, and I promptly smote him to smithereens.

Leaving the racket in his empty basin, I tried to whistle and traipse down the asphalt. My lips were too dry, my body too stiff. I merely tooted air through my lips and walked with a twitchy gait.

28

THE LABYRINTH WITHIN THE STORM comprised
an endless loop of erratic chaos that went on and on,
revolving and evolving.

There was no way out.

Yet paths could converge and did, whether
Anzillu wanted them to or not. In his teasing and
testing, the prodding and poking, he could not predict
what these humans would do. He could only guess,
make educated assumptions, based upon his
observances.

What appeared to be could be misleading, even
to a powerful semi-omniscient spirit such as himself.
And so he erred in judgement.

His little science experiment wasn't going quite
as he planned. It exasperated him that he was incapable
of controlling the outcome. With most, not all, he felt
vexed by their fortitude and resilience.

For them the events were transpiring in a brief
span of time, during a hurricane he had whipped up.
He was still outside the doorway of their building.
For him it seemed to be taking forever! He did not
possess infinite patience. Or wisdom.

Anzillu could slow and even halt Time. He could
create mind-bending illusions, perform Spatial Synthesis.

But he could not make them do what was not in
their nature. The humans were following their own
paths. Following their hearts.

29

I KNEW I WAS GETTING CLOSER, every pang of despondence and stitch of suffering along my route bringing me that much nearer to a destination I had come to associate with far more than just finding assistance. (Or, in all likelihood, waking from a wild nightmare with chills and a headache.) Still, I wasn't sure I could make the distance. Physically I was a wreck. Emotionally I was a wreck that had been run over by a train. Perhaps sandwiched between two head-on colliding trains.

I frankly didn't know how much more I could tolerate, even with a magic bag. Finding out about my aunt shook me to the core. I had suppressed a disturbing childhood incident. Now that I knew the truth, I didn't know how I could face her. I no longer wished to call her. Who *would* I contact? I had no-one else. It's a terrible thing to be so alone.

But then I gleaned I was not alone. The initial hint was a giggle and I panicked, fearing the trees had unrooted and were trailing me on the road, where I had perceived I was safe from them!

Next I heard rustlings and rattles. That was odd. It didn't sound like trees. Should I stop and turn? Wouldn't that be the normal thing to do? I was reticent to provoke whatever was behind me. On this highway, it could not be something welcome.

Establishing that precept, I accelerated my pace. The covert noises increased, as if my stalker was speeding up too. I had to discern what I was dealing with, how nasty it would be, so I threw a glance over my shoulder. And froze in bafflement.

A mob of trick-or-treaters the size of small children scurried after me. They weren't what I was expecting. Not that I knew what to expect, but they didn't seem very threatening. I almost relaxed.

Until the doubts piled up. What were kids doing out here at night? Where did they come from? Why would they trick-or-treat along a highway instead of in their neighborhood?

And why would they trick-or-treat when it wasn't even Halloween?

I didn't *think* it was Halloween. Did I lose track of time?

The little buggers started running toward me. Were they scared? Did they want help? If so, they were in for a disappointment. I was the last person who could help them; I desperately needed some myself.

Forming a ring around me, the masquerading munchkins began to sing and skip with their hands clasped:

> When the moon is nice and bright
> That's when we come out to bite
> Trick-Or-Treat is such delight
> We do it every night . . .
>
> Candy kisses we demand
> Goodies, baddies, fill our hand
> Give us lovely contraband
> Our wish is your command . . .

We want your bitter and your sweets
All your bones and blood and meats
Best not be stingy with the treats
Or we'll eat your parakeets!

I didn't have a parakeet, but the words of their
song spooked me nonetheless. The voices were creepy,
their deportment undeniably occult. I was clearly in
for another hellstorm of iniquity! Just what I needed.
I rolled my eyes.

Feeling like a maypole, I was relieved when the
singing and circling ended. They were making me
dizzy. The evil trick-or-treaters proceeded to laugh
with great alacrity, then removed their masks.
What was underneath would have made a better
costume.

Their skin was warted, lumpen, pinkish-green.
They had squarish crooked teeth, overhanging brows.
Several of the midgetous creatures had bulbous
features and arbitrary tufts of hair. Others had
thick manes and beards, extrusive noses.

"Bet you thought we were children!" a bearded
shorty bantered. "We're hobgoblins!"

"And boggarts!" added the other type of dwarf.

"If you don't feed us, we're going to play tricks!"
the crusty lot of them chimed. "We may even eat *you*."

Okay, I'd had about enough of this! I'd already
gone through a nightful of garbage with a plenitude
of trauma thrown in. I didn't need a pack of wee
pranksters singing about eating pet birds or wanting
to eat me, for that matter!

Scowling, dredging in the bag at my side,
I discovered a single piece of chocolate-caramel candy
in gold cellophane. Was I supposed to give it to them
and let them fight over it like the plum? Or was I meant
to eat it myself?

The Werebear

My stomach decided for me. I unfolded the wrapper.

The dwarves clamored, hopping to grab it. Quickly I popped it in my mouth and chewed. They clawed at me in rage. The chocolate caused my belly to ping and groan, emit embarrassing sounds. I placed a hand over my abdomen. Nothing useful was happening. Maybe I shouldn't have eaten it, I should've given it to them!

The hobgoblins and boggarts wanted to tear me apart. They dragged me to the pavement. I had done the wrong thing. I wasn't going to make it. Hapless and forlorn, I gaped up at their cruel expressions.

My body itched. Fur sprouted. Bones and features distended. My clothing was taut, stretching. I could see my hands had become paws. There was hair on my face. Was I —?

"A werebear!" hollered a boggart.

The hobs and bogies dashed willy and nilly.

Whatever I was, I felt strong and self-assured like never before. Rising with a ferocious bellow, I frightened the shrimps out of their costumes. They scattered to the woods abandoning their guises, yet greedily clutching their precious sacks of candy.

The danger was past. I grew back to myself, smoothing and shedding. I hoped the trees would chastise those wretched dwarfs!

A few candies lay on the asphalt. Ignoring temptation, I trudged onward. I'd had my fill of enchantment.

30

TONKA AND JUNIPER bounced on a squishy flowerbed
damp from recent storming. Rhonda and Terence broke
their falls from the tightrope upon a cart laden with wet
straw. The four out-of-towners conspicuously thronged
in a deserted street. There were no cars or pedestrians.
Windows of stores were vacant of merchandise.
The visitors had skydived without parachutes into
a ghost town.

"Maybe it's siesta time," proposed Terence.

"Only if they take two-year naps," uttered Rhonda.
She had stepped to the sidewalk and was reading the
date on a yellowed newspaper in a metal box.

"Nobody lives here," Juniper stated. "Nobody *alive*,
dat is."

"Let us see if we can find our friend." Tapping his
magician's hat with the wizard wand, Tonka led the way
through the streets. It was a small burg. There was no
sign of life. Even the stray cats and dogs were missing.

"What if she's inside one of the buildings? Or
a house? Maybe she's taking a nap," Rhonda offered.

"Like Goldilocks!" piped Terence.

"Her hair isn't gold!" quibbled Rhonda.

"What color is it then?" Terence demanded.

Rhonda paused. "I can't remember."

"Does anyone recall?" asked Juniper.

The four of them looked blank.

"We are beginning to forget," Juniper sadly
conceded.

"I have spent too much time forgetting," Tonka deplored.

"It will happen," said Juniper. "Soon we will forget her. And she will forget us. And we will forget each other. We will move on, as all energy must."

"Are you sure that's how it works?" Rhonda quizzed.

Juniper nodded. "Dat is how my moder explained it to me."

"What if we don't forget? What if we remember this forever?" Rhonda wistfully inquired.

"None of us knows for certain. We were sent back here too soon," agreed Juniper. "So dat is what we will have to find out. When we return."

"For now we must find Meezly!" invoked Tonka.

They entered a red brick house to search . . .

31

THE SUBSEQUENT LEG of my travels lured me once more from the road to the trees. No, I hadn't lost my hold on sanity, hadn't forfeited my grip on reality. The excuse was basal: I was starved, and there beside the turnpike was an orchard containing the ripest most-lush fruit I'd ever seen.

This grove of trees lay to the left, whereas I had continually been drawn to the right side of the highway. That, too, was a compelling reason to risk.

My positive outlook, my inclination to hope for the best could entice me to fling caution to the breeze and trust Fate to guide my footsteps.

Besides, after the plum, I had a craving for a piece of fruit. Sometimes a need like that can build into a rift that devours its edges from the force of the necessity. If not satisfied, it may spread into an aching void of overwhelming combined needs that can never be sated. Or it might dull the whetted appetite of anticipation to a jaded hollowness too late to be appeased.

The orchard provided a bountiful assortment. Elatedly, as slivers of rain descended like gems in the moonlight, I roved across the highway and marveled at the abundance. There was tremendous joy in the act of picking a plum from a branch; especially when it represented the very thing you desired above all in that instant. A simple need fulfilled is a powerful thing.

Cupping my palms, I collected water and rubbed my hands together. Then reached for a wet purple sphere. Sinking my teeth with a smile into the skin and pulp, juice trickling down my chin, I savored the richness of the moment.

That funny sensation came over me, like when I turned into a lacewing, later a bear. My molecules were abuzz. But this time the metamorphosis was less extreme. Instead of my D.N.A. altering, my cells aged. Wrinkles and brown spots developed in the space of a breath. Fingers sought confirmation on my face. Flesh had thickened and sagged. My hair turned white.

I would be afraid to eat a plum from that day forward.

Rather than consult the bag, I raced — slowly — to a different tree and strained to pluck a yellow pear. There had to be a remedy, like an anti-toxin! Hand shaking, I lifted the pear to my mouth and took a bite. Chewing, I swallowed the piece of fruit and waited. It wasn't reversing.

Perhaps it wasn't enough.

I bit again, masticating at a leisurely rate, whereas ordinarily I ate too fast out of tension. And shrank to three-feet high. Now I was old and too small to reach the fruit on the lower branches! As usual, everything was going wrong.

Geriatric and diminutive, I doddered to a kumquat tree about ten feet in height. Stretching on my toes, I could nearly touch one of the yellow-orange ovals. Pulling my bag off, I cast it as a net holding the strap. A piece of fruit cascaded to the mud.

Grunting with a hand on my lower spine, I angled down then allowed the rain to rinse the kumquat.

A taste of sweet rind and sour pulp. Feeling
the crush of years — my age spots had age spots —
I swallowed peel and all. The effect was immediate.
A volcanic pressure on my forehead. Something
protruded. Raising a hand, my fingers discovered
the contours of a nose! This wasn't going well at all.

Under a cherry tree I swiped the bag. I should
have tried wishing for a net, but I didn't think the sack
would listen. Anyway, I was in a hurry, anxious to
undo the changes before my ticker's warranty expired.
A cherry bounced on grass. I shuffled after it.

Red polka-dots freckled my skin. At least the
brown spots were less visible. I examined the veiny
backs of my hands. I sure wasn't getting any younger.
I was afraid to keep biting the fruits, yet more afraid
to stop!

Hobbling to a banana tree, I thought: *Maybe
I need some potassium.* A bunch broke off when
I swatted the bag. I stripped and ate a couple for
good measure. My stomach was complaining.

Oh boy, what had I done now? Dire
repercussions occurred. My body vibrated like
a steaming boiler about to blow. Breath bated,
I dreaded the consequences. It seemed my blood
was curdling; rivulets of sweat bathed my flesh.
Then I inflated, puffing outward. Weightlessly
I started to float. My soles left the earth like
a departing spirit. Tugging the bag's strap over
my head and shoulder, a tight squeeze, I flipped
and yelled and struggled for an even keel.

Drifting by an apple tree, I acquired one and
took a chomp. Repulsed, I spat out the mouthful
upon seeing that the inside of the apple was dark
and wormy. "Eeeew!" An unpleasant aftertaste
lingered. To erase it, I glommed a peach in passing
and smelled the fuzzy fruit. It seemed okay. I sank
my teeth, leaving indents.

The nectar bled, sweet and succulent. The inner portion was a ripe orange-red. I bit off a chunk. Before long, there was something going on with the back of my head.

A third eye manifested. Blinking, I now had a rear view. It was kind of neat, and more useful than the second nose on my brow. Lazily somersaulting in the air, I paddled to a canopy of branches and leaves and — *cookies?* "Wait a minute, cookies don't grow on trees!" I protested. But they looked pretty yummy so I snatched a few handfuls. (I had grown a third hand along with the extra eye and nose.) Peanut-butter and chocolate-chip; with coconut, the way my mother had made them! I gobbled enthusiastically.

Too many cookies made me ill. I turned green, in fact. I must have looked rather peculiar with so many physical defects.

Orbiting a fig tree, I selected a sample and chewed. It was delicious. And they were said to have amazing properties. Could this be my cure-all? Fingers crossed, I waited. My bellyache disappeared. My feet met the ground. I percolated. My body spazzed. Oh yes, I was changing! The beauty flaws cleared. The polka-dots and additional parts vanished. But I did not grow taller. Not that I was so tall in the first place.

Disappointed, I grinned at my young hands. A person can feel bad and good the very same instant. At least I wasn't two hundred years old. I was grateful for that. But I realized my hands were a little *too* young — smaller as well. Apparently I was a child!

I was out of fruit. I had tried each type in the orchard. My only hope to come out of this normal was to reach for whatever the bag could conjure. My fingers explored its parameters corner to corner. "No! Come on!" My voice was frantic.

As I was about to withdraw my hand, a knuckle bumped an object. Removing it, I beheld a pill . . . Individually wrapped, the tablet bore tiny letters: CURE-ALL.

Peeling open the square, I hesitated. What was it, exactly? And did it intend to be swallowed or chewed? I had to decide and I was so tired. I popped the pill while debating the issue. I didn't need to do either, for it quickly dissolved. Unfortunately, it seemed to be a placebo instead of a panacea. I was still a child and felt more helpless than ever.

At that moment the trees of the orchard waged a blitzkrieg, pelting me with soft or rotting fruit. I had to flee to the blacktop then escape down the highway, coated by the splattered semblance of a bloody massacre.

32

THE THREE UNFRIENDS mungled to a door marked
DEAD END. Spiro wanted to see what was on the
other side. He balked at many things, but not at being
an ignoramus. He was more than willing to do that.
Driscoll had changed his mind; he was bored. What
started as entertainment had grown tedious. He was
sick of the plaintive puling of the pheebophobic lummox
and wanted to feed him to a rabid barracuda (being that
the ninny was afraid of fish). The battle-axe was just
plain irritating. He wanted to tape her mouth shut
full of incensed hornets. But he wasn't sure how to
find his way home, and he was hoping that one of
them knew. He was out of his element. Still, he
couldn't pass up a chance to heckle the dork.

"I suggest you rush through with your eyes
closed."

"Maybe I will," umbraged Spiro. "And maybe
I won't. Did you ever think of that?"

"You don't even make enough sense to *not* make
sense!" Driscoll barbed.

Missus Drager was fed up with both numskulls.
They were sidetracking her, arguing about a useless
door. "You clowns shut up!" the woman badmouthed.
"We've got to keep going! We can't worry about a stupid
door that doesn't go anywhere!" To prove it, she grasped
the knob and pulled it wide. "See? I'll show you!"

Minerva stepped through. The dead end actually
did go somewhere. Down. And it kept going, all right,
because it was dead and Death has no end.

She would never be seen again.

The guys peered after her. Oh well. Spiro
slammed the portal. They walked on till there was
a door marked DO NOT ENTER. That was just asking
for it, Spiro believed. Nobody told *him* what to do, so
he entered. A large unruly behemoth — which is similar
to a woolly-mammoth moth — resided on the other side,
and it had a man-sized appetite. He was a man about
the size of a man, so it ate him.

Driscoll fancied himself more clever than most,
and he wasn't going to be opening any doors any time
soon. That's why he encountered a chair labeled
SIT HERE. A chair isn't a door and he didn't see
the harm, so he sat. And he sat. It spared him
from having to wonder what might happen if he didn't.
He was waiting instead to find out *why* he should sit.

Waiting could be excruciating torture.
Particularly the kind of waiting where you could
do nothing else or you might miss what you were
waiting for. Driscoll Wunderbar couldn't stop waiting,
or wondering. He was afraid to get up even a second
because if he wasn't sitting there waiting when the
answer finally came, it might not stop. Like waiting
for a bus.

If he thought he was bored before he sat down,
he had another think coming. This boredom had no
limit. It had no bottom. It went on and on.

But he couldn't know that. He would keep
waiting with expectation. And that made it all the
more unbearable . . . due to being ever so slightly
tolerable.

33

HERE I WAS, the apprehensive little girl who had lost
her confidence many moons ago on another terrifying
night of wind and rain. It was all coming back to me
as I ran — from the trees and the past. Camille's
treachery led me to wonder what she was up to now,
being so solicitous, handling the estate paperwork.
Insisting that I needed to rest and recuperate from
the shock of losing my parents; telling me not to worry
about anything. It all rang false. What I confessed to
the witch was true. I suspected my aunt of colluding
with the doctor she had promised would help me!

Once that knowledge became firm, each step
gained assurance. Each stride grew lengthier.
My second childhood rapidly flew by and I found
myself normal. As normal as someone can be who
has been through what I have.

I slowed to a walk, lungs and throat raw, my legs
heavy. Hands on knees I panted, face warm, chest cold,
slathered in the detritus of a fruit-storm.

Betrayal was a twisted dagger. I needed to extract
the blade from behind me. It was out of my reach.

Drawing deep gulps of air, heart still racing,
I followed the road. What else was there to do? I was
caught up in the one-track-single-minded obsession
of moving forward. I couldn't turn around. I had come
too far in this direction, invested too much time and
energy. It was one of those situations. The only option
was to just keep going.

Embracing myself for comfort and warmth,
I briskly staggered along. I knew as sure as if I were
staring into a crystal ball that something preternatural
would assail me. It was that kind of day.

A rogue wind trickled beyond my hunched form . . .
gathered twigs, decaying leaves, dried grass and weeds.
A creature rose, assembled out of such debris, and stood
before my path. As he contemplated me, his joints were
knotted by serpentine vines. He was jagged, splintered,
shoddily constructed. But a drab aura of twilight
intensity surrounded him.

Facing this pillar of roughage, I had no fear.
I had no adrenaline. It was all depleted. I stared forth
in a fatigued state of readiness. I guess you could call it
confidence. Or craziness. Maybe it was both. I believed
not in myself but in my bag. A modest canvas sack.

The Rickety Man was poised like a gunslinger,
as if we were engaged in a showdown. A duel to the
finish. A clash of wills and won'ts. There was nothing
complicated about it. We were here because we had
to be. We had to do this. Although neither of us knew
why. He would draw his figurative six-shooter. I'd coolly
reach inside the bag. One of us would march away, the
other fall. It was a tale already written. We were letting
the scene play out.

"Wheeeeere?" A moaning wheeze sieved through
the effigy's frame.

For once I had no questions. Nor did I have the
answers. His stick hand went for it. My right hand
dove. My expression was stolid. He was a mere
obstacle. I was three miles from my goal. Unflinching,
unswerving, I refused to die by a nonexistent bullet
fired from an imaginary gun aimed by a quixotic man
of the mulch! There wasn't a trace of doubt in my mind,
however, that the menace was genuine.

Out of the bag I pulled a slat of wood. It was
shaped for throwing, like a boomerang.

There was no chance to think of rhetorical queries like *What if I miss?* and *What if it doesn't work?* I threw the stick.

End over end it reeled, and struck The Rickety Man about the level of a collarbone. If he had a collarbone. I'm not sure what he had but it snapped like a twig. Which it probably was.

It must have been a pivotal part of his anatomy. His head fell off. His torso and arms came undone. He clattered to Highway Zero, a pile of vegetation and wood. I felt my bravado crash with him.

Apathetic, barren inside, I kicked his remnants as I crunched by . . . enroute to Woebegone.

34

THE SNITTY NO-GOODS had been rebuffed into
a purgatorial zone where they were being dumped on,
chased and electrocuted by a Will-O-Wisp thunderstorm
that lit them up like neon signs. Camille and Nigel
scuttled in frenzied unremorseful terror, blaming each
other for getting them into this.

"You're such a quack! This is all your fault!
I should never have listened to your connivings,
insisting how foolproof and easy it was!" refrained
Camille.

"You're the one who wasn't satisfied bilking your
niece! You had to have some ridiculous stone!" was
Nigel's eternal lament.

Creatures were flung: eelish sea monsters with
fangs and kraken jaws; centipedal squids with razor
snouts, clawed appendages; lightning-snakes and
gremlins that glowed. The immensely self-involved
carpish couple did their best to dodge. As Nigel ducked
a sabertooth fish, it whapped Camille in the puss and
deflected to graze Nigel's ear. Camille batted a fly-by
vampire squirrel at her boyfriend, who eeked and
bunted it back like a ping-pong ball.

They were unprepared for such madness,
ill-equipped to cope against a barrage of paranormities
that had no place in a rational world. The pair lacked
sufficient valor to withstand the trials and throes
heaped upon them. Weak characters are apt to fold
when tasked to overcome adversity.

There was no recourse but to blubber, to come unwoven like a knit muffler and lose what dignity they thought they had.

35

TWO MORE MILES. I greeted the sign dispassionately, my endurance seriously flagging. I didn't know by then if I would ever be warm or dry or comfortable again. You can reach a state where you're so downright miserable that you're reduced to a needy child, hugging and babbling to yourself. Courage can waver. Determination can falter. It seemed a lifetime since my journey commenced in search of the stone. I was no closer to finding it, and had managed to lose my friends. Would I ever see them again? At the moment I was so destitute, so wrung out and exhausted through and through that I harbored little capacity to even worry about their whereabouts.

And yet, one thing I learned on this little adventure was how much I needed friendship, affection, the support of family. Without these factors in my life, what was there? What mattered?

The things people have strived for, fought and killed over — the power; the fame and fortune; land and luxuries — are so meaningless and shallow without loving, without being loved. It is absolutely imperative to appreciate this and not let it go or take careless risks once you have found love. Or it finds you.

I knew this in my heart and mind, even within my soul. But I honestly could not feel anything. I was simply numb. And in such a state, I couldn't find the wherewithal and balance to handle what came next on that stormy night.

Displaced feelings would be pitted against me, turned into creatures that would attack and rend my tattered spirit.

The first to lash out was Anxiety. Rearing aloft, the Tyrannosaurus Rex of emotions, this terrible tyrant thumped towards me on raptor toes and unleashed a vicious howl that resonated down to my own toes and sounded like a question.

I didn't realize this was the beast that had been surfacing in me at times of stress. How could I defend myself from an entity so fierce? Despite months of therapy sessions with Doctor Hurst, I was no better off. My parents were still gone, and I still had the same underlying tensions.

Now, though, I had come to recognize that Aunt Camille and her friend Nigel were treacherously plotting to do the opposite of heal my troubles. That's why my nose often itched in their presence. I had overlooked it, brushed it aside. With this knowledge, perhaps I had the power to defeat the monster. I was becoming an experienced monster-slayer, after all.

Standing my ground, straddling the centerline of the highway, I stared down Anxiety. The beast shuddered across pavement, quivering with the desire to trample me. I had no fear — but soon I would face that also.

Self-preservation can be a stout ally. Fingers scrabbled inside the bag. I scooped a handful of dust. What was it for? The texture informed me it was sand. Calmly I tossed the powder. And was swept from the road by the beast's tail. The T-Rex was blinded. His stampede careened. His bulk concussed.

Picking myself up, I regained my feet. Fear and Doubt, Panic and Paranoia materialized as a four-headed slime demon. The pink and pea-green beast absorbed Anxiety. A fifth head emerged from its mucosive midst.

Good feelings — Love, Respect, Compassion, Confidence and Trust — hovered like wraiths. The slime monster snuffled towards them.

Lacking the typical reactions we take for granted, I could only reach into my bag of tricks wearing a deadpan expression. I wasn't sure a fistful of sand would suffice. My hand found something different. Nothing.

What did that mean? Biting my lower lip, I postulated that it might be up to me to confront my fears, exorcise my demons. Maybe that's what the bag was trying to tell me. That I needed to believe in myself. I didn't need pills to control my anxieties. I needed to find the stability and stamina within. I needed to not panic or stress out, not give in to worry and pressure.

Or maybe the bag just ran out of tricks. I held it open, turned it upside down and shook. Still nothing.

I wasn't in the mood for introspective life lessons. I needed a solution, or that slime thing was going to suck in my positive feelings and use them against me too!

The icky beast was slow, but the good vibes were clustered together. I tried to shout at them to run. My voice caught in my trachea. The slime creature swooshed in a blink of the eye and was ingesting the wraiths.

A ten-headed monster started making a snail-trail for me. I did all I could do right then: limp away, as fast as I was able!

36

RICHARD GOURD AMBLED down Main Street. After
all he had seen, it was not very strange that this haven
should be so quiet. Or that it was so desolate. The odd
part, he thought, was that it should be here in the middle
of this craziness. Yet he sensed there was something
beneath the fraudulent mantle of stark beguiling
sereneness: an ugly truth waiting to be unveiled.

As a detective, he had seen his share of devious
people. Some of them, like the town, hid behind
pleasant smiling exteriors. They said the right words
to make themselves be liked, precisely what gullible
people wanted to hear, so they could infiltrate and
manipulate the lives of others. They were wolves
cloaked as sheep.

He had arrested depraved individuals who were
too far from normal to ever go back — if they were ever
there at all.

Gourd had poked his head in the lion's mouth on
many occasions, treading a thin line between the ethics
of morality and getting the job done. He had crossed
that line in the interest of preserving peace, bringing
to justice those who made streets like this unsafe.

During his years on the force, he had developed
an unerring instinct about the darkness in men's souls.
What his gut told him about this community, as he
scrutinized its heart, was that evil had resided here.
And perhaps still did.

37   .

THE FINAL STRETCH — a mile from town — I had
a slime beast in tepid pursuit, visible in the distance
thanks to a brilliant sheen of illumination, although
I could distinguish no moon in the cloud-covered
heavens. Recalling its sudden-speed maneuver,
I walked brusquely trying to stay well ahead.

 I couldn't feel relieved that I was so close to
civilization, or that salvation might be imminent.
I couldn't feel much of anything. I didn't care what
fresh calamity was in store for me either.

 You can't go through what I did in so short
a timespan without thoroughly draining your
adrenal gland. Fatigue had graduated to exhaustion.
How I managed to retain my footing and put one in
front of the other is something of a mystery.

 It wasn't long before I began to smell the acrid
scent of smoke. Around a curve in the road I saw
gray clouds rolling towards me and the orange light
of flames. Was the forest burning? Was the town
burning too? I increased my pace, a hand to my
mouth. Clearing the bend, I witnessed not a firestorm
in the trees but upon the highway itself.

 How was it fueled? And it seemed to be moving
in my direction!

 I retreated. Then remembered I could not go
back. I had come too far. And the path wasn't clear.

 Great, now I had a slime beast at my back and
a fire monster ahead! Not to mention being flanked
by unfriendly trees! I was in quite a predicament.

The burning beast advanced. I could make out arms and legs, a head. He was towering, a reddish-orange giant with flecks of yellow. Glancing over my shoulder, I could see my feelings approach. What was I going to do? My right hand plunged into the sack but the magic had failed me, so I didn't give out much hope it would save me from an impossible situation! As expected, the bag was empty.

Of the woods emerged a familiar giant: I felt his footfalls shake the ground, then the pines at the forest fringe swayed and Green Man stepped through.

Fantastic! I was really cooked now! Proving it, the fire hellion hissed up to me and raised his arms in a menacing pose, vehemently roaring. The heat he radiated singed my lashes and brows. His steps seared the pavement with scorchmarks.

Green Man frowned and extended a hand. I screamed. To my surprise, the forest lord gently lifted me onto his shoulder. With a deep huff, he blew out the flames. The monster was extinguished like a candle.

Setting me down, the giant harrumphed: "This isn't over! There will be no forests left if we do not send a message to your kind. The reckless destruction of our communities must end, for your sake as well as ours! You do not know what you are damaging, the magnificence and intelligence that exists in these woods, and the pain you are causing! Nor can you imagine all that is being lost before it has been discovered! The forest is a vast and intricate network linked around the globe. We communicate through the roots in the soil. Through fibers and waters and winds. I can wake up in any forest because I am a part of them all. They are my children. If you heed nothing else, be aware that all is one. The sky, the land, the sea. Hurt any part of it and you hurt yourself."

Regarding my emotional slime — which was drawing near and grumbling in a high-pitched slur of voices — Green Man chortled, "*That* you will have to deal with *alone*." He pounded back into the trees.

Alone. I was alone with my feelings. And feeling alone in the world. Standing there, heart gonging in my breast, drawing gulps of air to reduce the redness of my cheeks, I wet my ragged parched lips wanting to cry. Yet I could not even release the tears and sorrow in my eyes for this day. For the past year. For the revelations and losses I had not allowed myself to feel, even when I had feelings.

Was I losing everything along this route? My last shred of identity and emotion? Would I be as devoid as the number implied when I reached the end of Highway Zero?

The answer impended like an evasive memory that capers on the brink of cognizance. Every feckless clumsy tromp delivered me nearer. It was the last leg of the odyssey and I was on my last leg.

But the wooded ones were not going to let me off that easy. A lynch crew of deciduous gangsters rimmed the road, a gaunt double death squad, their leaves shunned as a dog expels water from fur, bony tentacle talons flogging and drubbing the air, endeavoring to pulverize me. After all I had perversely been subjected to, it seemed the most enervating, demoralizing, unhinging sight . . . those truculent boughs absent foliage against a doleful sky. A noose-knotted branch squirmed out to string me up. Trees can certainly hold a grudge. From the canopy came a resounding *ahem*, and the insurgents ebbed to the forest-line with a harangue of sappy sullen oaths.

Listless strides petered; breath clogged a constricted windpipe. Even the rumpus of trees couldn't penetrate my dreary torpid brume. I was unimpressed. "Nice try," saluted an austere vagabond. "You almost had me there."

The Road To Woebegone

38

WELCOME TO WOEBEGONE, proclaimed a placard at the edge of town. Arletta Trimble, known to most as Meezly, wandered past the sign bereaved and dazed. A voice kept repeating one word in her brain: *Where?* She paid it no mind. She didn't know. Didn't even know the rest of the question — the *what* attached to the where. Just as she didn't know *who* she currently was, only that she wasn't herself.

The black-haired woman, who now had locks of white on each side of her shoulder-length tresses, dithered over leaving the highway. It had been all she could count on during the sojourn here. She was shivering from cold and trauma, from the drought of emotions within. Sniffing, hugging herself, Meezly surveyed the township's main thoroughfare. No activity was discernible.

The slime monster continued to shamble in her wake. What was it waiting for? Why didn't it speed up and grab her, get it over with? She shook her head. "Whatever."

She was beyond concern. Funny how the events of a single day could drastically warp your perspectives and priorities. Everything you thought was true . . . Everything that seemed presently important . . . Everything you envisioned for the future. It happened to her a year ago. And it was happening again.

Meezly drew a breath and set foot inside the town.

Initially it was discreet motions, subtle fleetings.
Then she gandered a figure. The girl from the graveyard.
A pale apparition, raccoon eyes. What was the name?
She pictured the tombstone: Belinda Ogden.

Why was she seeing a dead girl? Was it another
gift, along with the nose and her intuition? The girl
must be a restless spirit. What did she want? Meezly
considered asking, but wasn't sure if a ghost could have
a conversation. And if so, if she could see dead people
and talk to them, why didn't she see her parents?
Wasn't there anything they wanted to tell her?

"Belinda?" Meezly tested.

The girl was closer, then flitted back to the
entrance of an alley between buildings. She turned
and was gone. Did she wish to be followed? Meezly
shrugged, crossing the street.

At the alley she peeked in. The girl was waiting
farther down. "What is it? What do you want to show
me?" No response. Meezly pursued her into the dark
passage, blindly groping her way. "Where are we going?"

She jumped in fright, noticing a white translucent
form beside her. The girl was in an open doorway.
Meezly cautiously entered the building and trailed the
spirit to a staircase for the basement level. The building
was eerily lit by blue and green phosphorescent fog stains
on walls, floor, and ceiling. She ventured to the bottom,
the girl drifting ahead. They progressed along a corridor.

Through a supply room with shelves, they traversed
to a maintenance shaft of exposed wires and pipes.

The ghost led Meezly to an opening where a large
square grating was affixed. The girl gestured. Meezly
crouched to extricate the grill. The metal plate caused
a loud echo. Meezly clambered into the space on hands
and knees, emerging in a quarantined vault at the end
of which was a metal door. The wraith posed beside it,
her face pleading.

Meezly walked to the door, nose tingling, her spine too. There was something truly creepy about this, she thought. Pulling the heavy iron slab, she stuck her head into a black chamber and listened to the silence.

Then she percepted a faint stifled whimper.

"Hello?" Her voice was amplified.

Another cry, less muted.

"Who's there?" Meezly hailed.

Silence. A girl's shy voice: "Penny."

Meezly felt a jolt of recognition. She had blurted something to the witch about finding Lucky Pennies! On impulse, her hand slipped into the bag. She gripped a cylindrical object.

Sliding a button, Meezly searched the darkness with a flashlight beam until the ray discovered a teen with a copper-colored mane huddled on the floor. One of her ankles was tethered to the wall by a chain hooked to a ring.

Hurrying to the girl, comforting her with a hug, Meezly promised to get her out of there. "You're my Lucky Penny, and things will be better for us both from now on!" she pledged.

The chain was secured to a metal cuff fastened by a padlock. Closing her eyes, Meezly tried the bag. And came out with a gold key. Fitting it into a slot in the base of the lock, she released the girl's leg.

Penny's ankle had sores from the shackle.

"Come on!" Meezly helped the girl stand. Dressed in a filthy yellow teeshirt and grimy denim cut-offs, Penny gave her a peck on the cheek out of gratitude.

An arm around the teen, Arletta helped Penny from the vault. The girl had bare feet. They exited the grate shaft, made it to the stairs and climbed gradually.

Navigating to the alley door, Meezly invited the teenager to clasp her arms about her neck. Leaning forward, she grasped Penny's calves and straightened to carry her piggyback. Meezly staggered to the street. She wouldn't be able to tote the girl far, but hopefully they could locate someone else before long.

As they hove down the avenue, Belinda lifted a hand in farewell. They passed the ghost and Meezly smiled at her, but Penny was unaware.

Meezly looked up to see the street lined with other apparitions. Grayish-white girls without shoes, raising their hands as the survivor was lugged by. Arletta's orbs burned with tears. If she could feel, she would be sobbing her eyes out. This girl must have been the latest victim of a serial killer, and Belinda Ogden wanted Meezly to rescue her. But who would rescue Meezly? Thousands of steps had brought her to the town for that purpose, only to find a greater purpose: Penny. Yet they both needed saving!

Meezly squinted, catching a glimpse of a man strolling out of a house blocks away. Shouting "Hey!", she attempted to run. Instead she was forced to let go of Penny and sink to her knees, strength diminished.

The man veered onto the street then halted to observe them. His features were inscrutable at that range. When his steps resumed, they were swift and hard.

"Finally." Arletta could just watch the advent of help, her body throbbing with relief.

Penny was standing behind her. Gasping, the teen fervently tugged at Meezly to rise. "It's him! It's him!"

Comprehension was sluggish. Meezly's eyes narrowed. The man didn't appear big and bad. He didn't seem scary. Why was the kid so upset?

It dawned like an eruption of sun. In the end, the worst monster she would meet seemed like an average guy.

He was sprinting now; his head was bullet-shaped, his curls brown, his face unremarkable. He could have been anybody, an Everyman.

Except that he was a stone-cold murderer and child abductor. He had slain all of the children of this cursed town barring Penny, and the adults had moved away.

Arletta, too, was ready to get out of Looneyville. The maniac pounced before she could reach for some magic, punched her in the jaw. She was glad it wasn't her nose, which had done enough bleeding for one day and might have shattered, being fairly cold.

Meezly woke, trussed by the wrists and ankles on the floor of the guy's house. Penny lay beside her, eyes wide, emitting pathetic whines. Joe Average sipped a can of diet cola, watching them from a kitchen stool, digging the tip of a blade into the top of a counter. He plodded over to Meezly in running shoes, then kicked her ribs.

"Who are you? And who sent you?" the creep interrogated.

"F.B.I.," Meezly hoarsed for the heck of it.

"Where's your badge?"

"Must've dropped it."

"What's the number?"

"They're numberless now. They use hieroglyphs," she teased. "Mine's a turtle and a cow."

The doorbell rang. Joe Average spilled his soft drink on his shirt. Sneaking to a window, he peered out the curtain. He probably didn't get many visitors, living in a ghost town.

The man snipped off strips of duct tape with the knife and sealed the mouths of his prisoners.

Charging to the door, checking that his captives would not be visible, he jerked it open a crack. Four spiels assaulted him at once.

"We'd like to borrow a cup of tea!"

"We'd like to give you a brochure on termite protection!"

"We're selling candy to raise funds for orphans!"

"We're selling Girl Scout cookies!"

The canvassers paused, then babbled that they were there for all of those things.

"You left out Holy Rollers!" Average Joe slammed his door.

The bell again. He wrenched the door wider.

"Can we interest you in a religious pamphlet?" the female with purple hair questioned.

"Get lost!" The serial killer glared at the group and closed his door.

Ding-dong. Teeth gritted, saliva foaming, he yanked it ajar.

"We are already lost. We need directions," the Frenchman in a hat requested.

"And we've lost someone. Have you seen her?" the African woman expressed.

Meezly was overjoyed to hear the voices of her friends. She made mumbling sounds, then kicked her heels against the floor.

"What's that?" The chick in red craned her neck to see past the door.

"I have pets," fibbed the killer.

"What kind?"

"Gerbils."

"They must be big," the pesky girl snooped.

"They're Giant Gerbils," he improvised.

"Interesting. I've never heard of them," she parried.

"I have to go — feed them now," he stammered. And shut the door in her face.

Livid, the guy stalked to Meezly and aggressively booted her ribs.

He went to the window and peeked. They were still at the door. The hat man was trying to spy in through the peephole.

Then another man showed up on the stoop and rapped with a fist.

Joe Average tore open the door. *"What?"*

An intense dark-haired man with a scarred brow introduced himself as a cop. The other four were behind him. "I'm looking for a young lady," intimated the detective.

"I live alone," said the serial killer.

Strange moans and thumps were audible.

"Just me and my gerbils," the guy amended.

"Mind if I look around?" the cop asked.

"Do you have a search warrant?"

"No."

"A badge?"

"No. I'm undercover."

"Then I do mind." Average Joe shut his door.

Springing into action, unlashing their feet, he escorted the prisoners to a rear door. The guy herded them over the backyard and escaped with them via two loose boards in a wooden fence.

The serial slayer ushered the females roundaboutly to Main Street. They were traveling along the opposite sidewalk when the detective and the door-to-door peddlers spotted them. Joe Average whisked out his blade and pressed it to Meezly's throat, pinning her against him with his other arm.

"Don't come any closer!" he warned.

Richard Gourd drew his gun in a two-handed stance.

Juniper, Rhonda, Terence, and Tonka obligently sidled instead of forward steps. "Use de wand!" urged Junebug.

Tonka flourished the rod, but there was no energy. "It isn't working."

Penny stood helpless beside Meezly and the serial killer as the street filled with specters. His dead victims glowered. Only Average Joe and Meezly were conscious of them. "Stay back!" He pointed his knife defensively.

The ghosts crowded inward, Belinda at the front.

Joe Average swung his blade to Meezly, sweating, eyes haunted. Gourd took a shot to save her. His bullet missed its mark. Taking advantage of the distraction, Meezly bashed her cranium against the killer's visage. He roared and raised his knife to stab her. The next bullet was accurate. The killer toppled with a hole in his head.

Meezly's friends cheered.

Sallying through spirit matter, scattering the dead girls, Gourd hastened to unbind the living ones. He was astounded to feel moisture on his cheek — that he could finally shed a tear!

Arletta gazed up and saw for the first time a good guy, not a villain. He saw her for the first time as an attractive woman rather than just a "girl". Their years were but a dozen apart. They experienced a mutual surge of admiration. A spark of connection. But Meezly was essentially hollow inside and turned away from him. He couldn't know this, couldn't understand that she was numb like he had been. His heart was pierced by a dagger-thrust of dolor.

The flock of victims dispersed into fragments, then vanished as the lost souls ascended to a state of peace. Their spirits could rest. Belinda lingered to exchange smiles and touch Arletta's hand in farewell.

Juniper told Meezly, "Soon it will be time for us to leave as well. Our forces have grown weak. And you will no longer need us."

"How could I not need you?" Meezly protested. "Where are you going?"

"We are ghosts too," explained Tonka. "You can just see us better."

"We were sent back to help you, Grace." Terence smiled.

"You know we'll always be with you — in your heart," Rhonda grinned. "Don't forget us."

"Yes, but you're all I have!" cried Meezly.

"Oh no, you have new friends now!" Junebug waved a hand at Penny and Gourd.

"Zere are always more to be found," encouraged Tonka.

"And we have a surprise!" Rhonda and Terence trumpeted.

Arletta couldn't imagine what might be more of a surprise than the fact they were ghosts. "What is it?" She expected something mind-boggling. She was not disappointed.

"Your parents are alive!" her four pals chorused.

"We discovered dem while looking for you," said Juniper.

"Zey have been inside zis storm!" annunciated Tonka.

Meezly couldn't believe her ears. Was it possible? She had learned today to think that anything and everything could be!

"Where are they?" she inquired eagerly.

"In the eye of the storm," Rhonda gloomily edified.

"And where is that?"

"You'll have to ask *him*," pointed Terence.

Behind her she was greeted by an image of the storm, a facsimile of the demon wind: a grayish swirling head and shoulders with bursts of light or dark; flashes of electricity that pulsed through the commotion.

Unbeknownst to Meezly, they had already met a number of times and places along her route to this moment.

Anzillu had taken many identities in order to test her mettle. He had developed a grudging respect for her, although he would never admit it.

"At last we meet — face to face and eye to eye," rumbled the storm.

"Could you tell me where to *find* your eye?" Meezly broached.

"An interesting inquest," the whirligig mused, "in that I might ask *you* the same!"

"My eyes are fairly obvious, I think."

"Are they? All of them? Are you *sure*?"

Meezly wondered what he was getting at. Just how many eyes did he suppose she had? "I think I would know if they weren't," said she.

"Would you? Then where is it?" thundered he.

"Why does everyone keep asking me that?" Meezly grouched.

"I keep asking," the demon clarified. "Me!"

"Okay, then where is *what*?" specified Meezly.

"The stone! The Cursed Eye!" flaunted Anzillu.

"That's exactly what *I've* been wondering!" she exclaimed. This must be what her father meant about safeguarding the stone! "Why do you want it?" she scowled.

"Why matters not, only where!"

"What would you do with it?"

"Tell me where!"

"I don't know, I don't have it," Meezly fessed.

"You must! And you will give it to me!" badgered the wicked windbag.

"I won't. It isn't yours!"

"You're wrong. You know nothing and you are nothing! You do not decide what is mine or not."

"The Eye was entrusted to me," stated Meezly.

"And I am its storm!" foisted Anzillu. "But I am not like those paltry temporal tempests that humans assign cute names, that blow over and dispel within days!"

He explained, "I was an evil minor spirit by birth. Until the stone made me a paradoxic anomaly — with both good and bad in one. I am unique."

"In *that* you are very much like humans," noted Meezly.

"I am not like anyone or anything!" Anzillu arrogantly blustered. "There is no counterpart to balance me, just the stone. When I rule that which rules me, I cannot be defeated. Except by the ultimate forces of Good and Evil. But they're too busy trying to outweigh each other to bother."

"If I had it, which I don't, I wouldn't give it to you!" Meezly defied.

The storm mustered up a snootful of puissance. "What you would or would not is of no consequence! You *shall* give it to me!" the typhoon raged.

It was a bluff. He couldn't make her. Enhanced by the stone, Anzillu could perform magical feats, but in many ways he was just an illusionist. He sculpted the air, yet could not create the rain or fire. He could only borrow them or manipulate clouds, generate flames with static and lightning. Nor could he conjure a solid. He had to distort matter, bend or break atoms, deceive the senses. He could wield pregnant clouds, pull up bodies of water and anything else he cared to unload. He could take miscellaneous objects and put them together, craft a diorama. He could manifest as any form, but it was a mere parlor trick. He needed to harness The Elements and he needed the stone for that, as well as to be his own master.

"I could crush every bone of yours in a single wiffet!" the mistral spited. "What makes you think you can oppose me?"

Bolstering herself, standing a little taller, Meezly answered: "I don't think any such thing. I am small and prone to lapses of courage or judgement. But I simply have to do what's right."

Pitching a tantrum, Anzillu sneezed a cascade of rain turning to snow freezing to ice upon her. Meezly had weathered such tribulations this night that a mere sneeze was unlikely to make her cringe. The zephyr coughed out a squall that flailed her hair yet did not make her wince. She was adamant in her resolve not to bend to the will of the storm.

"Very well. I have something you want, and you have something I need. Let us trade," bargained Anzillu.

Sopping wet and suffering chills, Meezly hesitated at making a pact with a devil. Still, if it was the only way to free her parents . . .

A spindly tall man with a gray brim and walking stick, tilted back as he strutted forth, tapped along the street and beckoned to Meezly: "Hey there, if you are in a perplexity of choice, a quandary of speculation, then it might be that I might just be just in time!"

Uncanting, the extraordinary feller spun his hat in a hand. "Mister Thaddeus I am, and I see you have arrived on the precipice of grayness, where not even the sun can shine for it slides right off. It is in the grayest of areas that we err as humans — where the mind can be confused, the heart distracted by the blurred and fudgy lines of facts, the obfuscated snarl of conflicting sentiments. Beware of the gray lest it seeps into you!"

He plopped his hat down on his dome and performed a grandiose bow.

"I am The Gray Man as you can see, and it is my honor to serve as your gondola-driver gendarme master-at-arms-length through these doldrums and straits of a troublesome or indecisive nature!"

Meezly blinked. "What's that again?"

"Nothing to worry about. Just follow my footsteps and we'll avoid the quicksand-trappings of the swampier gray regions. Let us begin at once!" Mister Thaddeus marched off with his funny way of walking.

Meezly, her brow furrowed, shrugged and trailed obediently at his heels.

The entire congregation of friends, acquaintances, storm demon and slime monster promptly tagged after.

The Gray Man sauntered up the street to a gray Victorian house, then pushed past the creaky iron gate of a low brick wall fencing the property. There he halted and waved his staff toward the front of the residence. "The eyes are the windows to the soul," saith he.

The proverb called attention to a pair of windows upon the face of the house. Meezly saw her mother and father, who seemed to be looking out from the inside. They were actually trapped within the panes.

Crying, she rushed to her mother and their hands met, glass between. The woman darted to her father in disbelief. They *were* alive! she rejoiced. But how could she free them?

"Do we have a deal?" bartered the storm.

Meezly's friends rallied with support, advising her to trust herself. Even Mister Gourd and Penny waited nearby with concerned expressions.

"You followed your heart all the way here. Do not stop now, for you are almost there!" extolled Mister Thaddeus. "The gray is neither here nor there. You can get lost in the gray and never choose, never take a side. Some things are black and white. Follow your heart."

"Some gray is good!" bandied the jinn. "Some gray is necessary!"

"For you gray is all there is!" reproached Mister Thaddeus. "Doing the wrong thing for trying to do the right thing is still wrong!"

Inspired by remembering her travails, Meezly checked if there was anything useful in the bag. She discovered a plain oval-shaped pebble.

What could she do with this, break a window?

The gray-white rock began to glow in her palm, adopting a greenish hue. Meezly understood then. It was crystal clear. She didn't need to find the stone; it found her. It was there all along, invisible, intangible, changing into objects.

The Eye Of The Storm clutched in her fist, she wished with all her heart for her parents to be safe. The stone did not respond.

A slime beast with ten heads waddled through the gate, scurried up behind her. She pivoted too late. Its upper appendages embraced her. Meezly thought she was finished, but it was the monster that merged into her. She wiped a film of ooze off her face.

Emotions intact, Meezly wished her wish a second time. Glass panes tinkled to the lawn and elated parents stood beside her. The family shared a warm reunion hug full of smiles and laughter.

Rhonda touched her shoulder. Meezly turned to behold the sad countenances of her friends.

"It is time," Juniper announced. "We will miss you."

"Don't forget!" Rhonda's bottom lip quivered.

"Olé!" Terence concurred.

Tonka beamed. "You will be fine. Keep believing in yourself. And magic!"

Hugging them, tears of happiness became tears of sorrow. "I love you guys!"

Drops pounded. A brutal gale ripped Meezly's beret from her head. She let it go this time. She was sobbing harder than the rain. Tonka had been like a father, and Juniper a mother. Rhonda and Terence were the siblings she had never known. The four quirky companions waved and walked out the gate. Their images faded. Meezly's weeping was drowned by the shower.

She had regained one family to lose another.

"Are you okay, dear?" asked her real mom.

"I knew you would find us!" her dad stated proudly.

Mister Thaddeus flicked his walking stick to a broad gray umbrella, doffed his hat and bid adieu, having more gray matters to attend.

The storm was angry. Crocodiles, tears and all, came out of the sky. They milled about in the yard, on the street, riled and bilious.

Drenched, Meezly and her parents joined Gourd and Penny. The frightened girl hugged Meezly, who met Richard's eyes.

"I'm glad you're safe," Gourd managed to get out.

A crocodile, jaws snapping, crawled towards them.

"Oh yeah, couldn't be better!" Meezly joked.

The town had lived up to its name, which ironically meant wretched or miserable.

For Penny and the other victims, the town represented Perdition.

To Richard Gourd, it symbolized Redemption.

For Meezly — who found her parents in it, found Penny and this man — it meant the *end* of woes. She thought that Woebegone fit just fine.

Bolts of lightning sizzled above.

A petulant demand boomed: "Give me The Eye!"

Steeling herself, the stone nestled in her grasp, Meezly confronted the demon wind.

Anzillu boasted that he was responsible for the Bermuda Triangle disappearances, for U.F.O. sightings and abductions. He had created tsunamis and hurricanes, tornadoes and blizzards. What chance did she have against him? She was just one tiny human!

Arletta held out her hand, uncurled her fingers. "This is just one small stone, and yet you fear it," she boldly scorned.

When she spoke again, it was the rock.

The Eye told the wind demon he had no place
in the natural order, for he was an unnatural force
like manmade bombs; like nuclear fusion and fission
in the hands of mortals. He was just as dangerous
as those he despised. The jinn had selfish motives
for protecting the planet, desiring to rule over the
natural and supernatural realms. He coveted
absolute power, but that would be the greatest
evil of all.

The stone released a blinding wave of light.
A tremendous percussion clapped like thunder;
the windworld shook. Rifts appeared in the town.
Crocs on the street slid into gaping cracks. Shops
and houses crumbled, sundering to plumes of dust.
Woebegone would just be gone.

The remaining visitors were abruptly swept out
of the storm's eye and dumped in the corridor of the
building where Meezly's adventure had commenced —
mere minutes before.

Denouement

BEING THE STONE'S KEEPER was an enormous
responsibility. I was still in the process of rebuilding
my confidence, and it would take time for me to adjust.
I went through some panic, thinking I wasn't strong
or capable enough. The stone was patient, as stones
usually are.

Richard was patient too. I had never been in love,
and that scared me more than being chosen by the
stone! Eventually I got used to the surges of euphoria
and exhilaration that accompanied love and respect
and the other nice feelings. In a couple of months
I got over the fatigue and recovered my balance.
I would still have twinges of anxiety, an occasional
bad dream. Who wouldn't after a night like that?
But happiness makes all the difference.

Speaking of happiness, Penny's family was very
happy to see her again. She and Richard and I formed
a special bond too.

My parents and I became closer, spending more
time together; drinking in the moments that can be
ignored or never happen with busy schedules and too
many distractions. I had declined before to globe-trot
with them, preferring to manage the website for the
family company. Abandoning my timidness,
I've started to foray with Jake and Lana on their
expeditions. I'm ready for the excitement, and
Richard loves to travel. But there's no place like
home.

Sometimes it takes a fantastical experience to appreciate the mundane and down-to-earth, the humbler aspects of existence. Life is a twisted path that can lead us through the most amazing adventures, then dump us right back where we started, wondering if we are better off or worse!

Richard was not the man I thought he was. It turned out he was a better man, a kind and caring man who didn't scare me anymore. He was allowing himself to be loved for the first time. He had always held back and not given himself completely.

Sometimes adversity can change everything. And sometimes the changes are good.

I do miss my friends, however. They were there when I needed them. When my aunt convinced me to check into a sanitarium after my parents died . . .

It was an asylum, she touted, where I could rest and recover without the pressures of the world. Camille had been conspiring with the director of the madhouse to steal my inheritance. But I wasn't the only one to be coerced into staying there (or involuntarily committed) who didn't belong in a loony bin. Rather than curing patients, Nigel was in the business of procuring and maintaining them to exploit for medical research and profit.

A television commercial had been produced to drum up business. Crawley Convalescent Home For Cuckoos And The Criminally Insane was advertised as a place for families to send their troubled loved ones. Also for people to commit themselves who just needed a break from reality, or Reality T.V.

The commercial depicted how beautiful the grounds were, and conveyed an atmosphere of healing and tranquility. It mentioned a nursery for insane babies who cried too much or had a toe fetish.

Tranquility was also the name of a street drug being manufactured there and given to patients illegally, along with being sold on the Black Market.

As the camera panned around, I could be seen conducting a discussion with four empty chairs in the day-room.

I resided on the minimum-security level for the "less violent" types. Upstairs were the wings for experiments, as well as the maximum-security wards. On the grounds was a petting-zoo enclosure that was supposed to be therapeutic for the patients, but was really a slaughterhouse and a way to smuggle out drugs to customers, stuffed in meat.

Richard was investigating Nigel, posing as a patient. After that night, the inmates who didn't belong were freed. Those who did require institutional care had been transferred to other facilities. It was too late for my friends. They were among the patients who died of abuse or neglect, from drug overdose or experimentation. The four of them had been sent back to haunt the place, both to be there for me and to help shut it down so their souls could rest. They additionally needed to learn what they had not learned in life about themselves.

They seemed so real. I thought they were. I could touch them. And they had touched my heart. Rhonda asked me to remember them. How could I not?

As for Camille and Nigel, their punishment would fit the crime. Driven insane, they were relegated to spending the rest of their days in padded cells. There's a cosmic law that applies: What goes around comes around.

In the real world, the supposedly *balanced* perch tentatively betwixt sanity's chokehold and the infirm reaches of what is so horrific or abysmal, so echoingly unfathomable, it leads to a state of mental paralysis.

I prefer to think we should all be a little nuts. Maintaining too tight of a grip, too much balance in an unbalanced world . . . that is true madness.

The story behind the story

Lori came up with the idea for *An Ill Wind Blows* upon accepting the challenge at the last minute to draft a novel in thirty days for a contest.

She won the Vicious Novel Writing Month award from Vicious Spirits. It might not be a major honor, but she was competing against some extremely talented authors and is very proud of her crystal trophy, as well as the book . . . which collected dust for more than a year while she worked on other projects, before finally being self-published. The only explanation she can offer on how intricate and articulate the story turned out under pressure, with so little time or chance to think, is that there was surely some magic involved with the writing of it.

Blackbirds were dropping from the sky in reality while this tale was being told. That detail wove its way into the tapestry straight from the news. The author had already heard of similar freakish occurrences regarding fish and the like.

An Ill Wind Blows contains a few references to *The Wizard Of Oz*. Lori states, "I did not have Oz in mind when I developed the plot and characters. Random elements merged together independently, including the cyclone: *Storm* was actually a prompt for the writing contest, and it fit flawlessly into the plot I had come up with two days before containing a fantasy realm, so I made the storm a character as well as the magical plane that the other characters would be drawn into. It was one of those things that seem to happen by cosmic design. After noticing the parallels to Oz, I decided to incorporate the references in tribute. But this is a far darker tale for the much older child in all of us!"

About the author

Lori R. Lopez embraces multiple genres in her prose and poetry — Horror, Humor, Fantasy and more. Her works range from book series to novels, short stories, and verse. She has published a broad selection of print and E-books including *Out-Of-Mind Experiences* (thirteen diverse tales); *Dance Of The Chupacabras* (Tome One of The Tome Trilogy Of Trilogies); *Chocolate-Covered Eyes* (a horror sampler); *The Macabre Mind Of Lori R. Lopez* (a horror collection); *An Ill Wind Blows*; and the chapbook *Keep The Heart Of A Child*, a witty volume of poetry and song lyrics as well as humorous and serious prose from the "Poetic Reflections" column published on her website: www.trilllogicinnoventions.com.

Fifteen of Lori's poems were featured for an anthology titled *In Darkness We Play* (Triskaideka Books). Her stories and verse have appeared in other anthologies such as *Mirages: Tales From Authors Of The Macabre* (Black Curtain Press), *Masters Of Horror: Damned If You Don't* (Triskaideka Books), *I Believe In Werewolves* (Netbound Publishing), *Soup Of Souls* (Panic Press), *Thirsty Are The Damned* (Rainstorm Press), *The Epocalypse: Emails At The End* (Pill Hill Press), and *Scare Package* (a charity anthology).

Proud of being a renegade author, she has developed her own unique vision and a variety of styles. It is her belief that creative writing should not be restricted by conventions. Taking this to heart, she generally likes to shake things up when it comes to the common rules of writing etiquette. And she goes to great pains to avoid redundancy as much as humanly possible. It's almost a little . . . nuts.

Lori has two sons and a pet polar bear. Okay, some of that's not true. She does have a pet peeve. Born in Wisconsin, she has lived in Hawaii, Florida, Spain and California but wants to live in a forest. She cares about conservation and wildlife and is an abuse advocate. She is also an artist and designs her own book covers. Lori has formed a creative company with her sons to publish books and record her songs, along with producing videos and independent films, among other goals.

The rest is *herstory*.

19713873R00146

Made in the USA
Charleston, SC
08 June 2013